Praise for Jhumpa Lahiri's

WHEREABOUTS

"[*Whereabouts*] signals a new mode for Lahiri . . . and an even more daring transformation. . . . [It's] true and wise to the core."   —*Los Angeles Times*

"[*Whereabouts* is] rendered in short, journal-like fragments so strongly and rightly voiced that other books sound wrong when you turn to them."
                                        —*The Atlantic*

"Lahiri writes with subtlety and delicacy."   —NPR

"Elegant. . . . Beautiful. . . . Lyrical."
                                        —*Pittsburgh Post-Gazette*

"As a stylist, Lahiri writes with grace, and has a talent for finding profundity in the ordinary."
                                        —*Chicago Review of Books*

"Without artifice, Lahiri's elegant phrases through-out the book reveal as much about her character as they do about the author's understanding of her environment and the people who inhabit it."
—*Minneapolis Star Tribune*

"A gorgeous, contemplative read. . . . Poetic prose that invites you to linger over the words."
—*Real Simple*

"A quietly bracing work of fiction. . . . [*Whereabouts*] is arguably [Lahiri's] most beautifully written novel."
—*The Nation*

"Lyrical and precise, Lahiri locates the vibrancy and bittersweetness of everyday life in the geography of one woman's footsteps."
—*Esquire*

"A delicately layered story. . . . It lends itself to being read in a single sitting, during which time you'll feel your own life standing still, suspended."
—*The Spectator* (London)

"This beautifully crafted novel is a stroll during the blue hour on the first warm evening of spring. . . . A jewel of a book."
—*BookPage*

"Elegantly observed and often beautifully sad, *Whereabouts* is a read that will stay with you longer than you anticipate."   —*USA Today*

"Hypnotic. . . . The book's peculiar magnetism lies in its clash of candor and coyness." —*The Guardian*

"Remarkable. . . . Deceptively simple, the language is powerfully controlled to render the greatest possible impact on the reader."   —*The Irish Times*

"A meditative and aching snapshot of a life in suspension. . . . Lahiri's poetic flourishes and spare, conversational prose are on full display. This beautifully written portrait of a life in passage captures the hopes, frustrations, and longings of solitude and remembrance."   —*Publishers Weekly*
(starred review)

"Painterly. . . . Exquisitely detailed. . . . [Lahiri's] language that seems to have been sieved through a fine mesh, each word a gleaming gemstone."
—*Booklist*

Jhumpa Lahiri

WHEREABOUTS

Jhumpa Lahiri is the author of four works of fiction: *Interpreter of Maladies*, *The Namesake*, *Unaccustomed Earth*, and *The Lowland*; and two works of nonfiction, *The Clothing of Books* and *In Other Words*. She has received numerous awards, including the Pulitzer Prize; the PEN/Hemingway Award; the PEN/Malamud Award; the Frank O'Connor International Short Story Award; the Premio Gregor von Rezzori; the DSC Prize for South Asian Literature; a 2014 National Humanities Medal, awarded by President Barack Obama; and the Premio Internazionale Viareggio-Versilia, for *In altre parole*. She was inducted into the American Academy of Arts and Letters in 2012 and named *Commendatore Ordine al Merito della Repubblica Italiana* (Commander of the Order of Merit of the Italian Republic) by President Sergio Mattarella in 2019. Editor of *The Penguin Book of Italian Short Stories*, she has twice been a finalist for the National Book Award, both as a novelist and as a translator.

WHEREABOUTS

——◆——

Jhumpa Lahiri

WRITTEN IN ITALIAN AND TRANSLATED
BY THE AUTHOR

Vintage Contemporaries

VINTAGE BOOKS

A DIVISION OF PENGUIN RANDOM HOUSE LLC

NEW YORK

Ad ogni mutamento di posto io provo una grande enorme tristezza. Non maggiore quando lascio un luogo cui si connettono dei ricordi o dei dolori e piaceri. È il mutamento stesso che m'agita come il liquido in un vaso che scosso s'intorbida.

—ITALO SVEVO, *SAGGI E PAGINE SPARSE*

Every time my surroundings change I feel enormous sadness. It's not greater when I leave a place tied to memories, grief, or happiness. It's the change itself that unsettles me, just as liquid in a jar turns cloudy when you shake it.

—ITALO SVEVO,
ESSAYS AND UNCOLLECTED WRITINGS

Contents

———

CONTENTS

Whereabouts

On the Sidewalk

In the mornings after breakfast I walk past a small marble plaque propped against the high wall flanking the road. I never knew the man who died. But over the years I've come to know his name, his surname. I know the month and day he was born and the month and day his life ended. This was a man who died two days after his birthday, in February.

It must have been an accident on his bike or his motorcycle. Or maybe he was walking at night, distracted. Maybe he was hit by a passing car.

He was forty-four when it happened. I suppose he died in this very spot, on the sidewalk, next to the wall that sprouts neglected plants, which is why the plaque has been arranged at the bottom, at the feet of passersby. The road is full of curves and snakes uphill. It's a bit dangerous. The sidewalk is vexing, crowded with exposed tree roots. Some sections are nearly impossible to negotiate because of the roots. That's why I, too, tend to walk on the road.

There's usually a candle burning in a container of red glass, along with a small bunch of flowers and the statue of a saint. There's no photograph of him. Above the candle, attached to the wall, there's a note from his mother, written by hand, encased in a milky plastic sleeve. It greets those who stop for a moment to ponder the death of her son. *I would like to personally thank those who dedicate a few minutes of their time to my son's memory, but if that's not possible, I thank you anyway, from the bottom of my heart,* it says.

I've never seen the mother or any other person in front of the plaque. Thinking of the mother just as much as the son, I keep walking, feeling slightly less alive.

On the Street

Now and then on the streets of my neighborhood I bump into a man I might have been involved with, maybe shared a life with. He always looks happy to see me. He lives with a friend of mine, and they have two children. Our relationship never goes beyond a longish chat on the sidewalk, a quick coffee together, perhaps a brief stroll in the same direction. He talks excitedly about his projects, he gesticulates, and at times as we're walking our synchronized bodies, already quite close, discreetly overlap.

Once he accompanied me into a lingerie shop because I had to choose a pair of tights to wear under a new skirt. I'd just bought the skirt and I needed the tights for that same evening. Our fingers grazed the textures splayed out on the counter as we sorted through the various colors. The binder of samples was like a book full of flimsy transparent pages. He was totally calm among the bras, the nightgowns, as if he were in a hardware store and not surrounded by intimate apparel. I was torn between the green and the purple. He was the one who convinced me to choose the purple, and the saleslady, putting the tights into the bag, said: Your husband's got a great eye.

Pleasant encounters like this break up our daily meanderings. We have a chaste, fleeting bond. As a result it can't advance, it can't take the upper hand. He's a good man, he loves my friend and their children.

I'm content with a firm embrace even though I don't share my life with anyone. Two kisses on the cheeks, a short walk along a stretch of road. Without saying a word to each other we know that, if we chose to, we could venture into something reckless, also pointless.

This morning he's distracted. He doesn't recognize me until I'm right in front of him. He's crossing a bridge at one end and I'm arriving from the other. We stop in the middle and look at the wall that flanks the river, and the shadows of pedestrians cast on its surface. They look like skittish ghosts advancing in a row, obedient souls passing from one realm to another. The bridge is flat and yet it's as if the figures—vaporous shapes against the solid wall—are walking uphill, always climbing. They're like inmates who proceed, silently, toward a dreadful end.

"It would be great, one day, to film this procession," he says. "You can't always see it, it depends on the position of the sun. But I'm amazed every time, there's something hypnotizing about it. Even when I'm in a hurry, I stop to watch."

"So do I."

He pulls out his cell phone. "Should we try?"

"How does it look?" I ask.

"No good. This contraption can't capture them."

We continue to watch the mute spectacle, the dark bodies that advance, never stopping.

"Where are you headed?"

"Work."

"Me too."

"Should we have a coffee?"

"I don't have time today."

"Okay, ciao, see you soon."

We say goodbye, separate. Then we, too, become two shadows projected onto the wall: a routine spectacle, impossible to capture.

In the Office

I t's hard to focus here. I feel exposed, surrounded by colleagues and students who walk down the hallways. Their movements and their chatter get on my nerves.

I try in vain to enliven the space. Every week I turn up with a shopping bag heavy with books from home, to fill the shelves. That pain in my shoulder, that weight, all that effort amounts to little in the end. It would take two years, three, to fill the bookcase. It's too capacious, it covers an entire wall. In any case, my office is now vaguely inviting, boasting a framed print, a plant, two cushions. And yet it's a space that perplexes me, that keeps me at arm's length.

I open the door, set down my bag, and prepare for the day. I answer emails and choose what book I'd like my students to read. I'm here to earn a living, my heart's not in it. I look through the window at the sky. I listen to some music. I read and correct student papers, and in so doing, I revisit the books I once loved so deeply. Occasionally a brave soul knocks on the door to ask my advice about something, or maybe a favor. The student sits in front of me, confident, full of ambition.

Given that I'm always coming and going, my thoughts can't manage to settle down here. My colleagues tend to keep to themselves, as do I. Maybe they find me prickly, unpleasant, who knows? We're forced to inhabit close quarters, we're told to be accessible, and yet I feel peripheral.

I gather that the colleague who used this office before me would sleep here now and then. I wonder, How? And where? On the floor, on a woolen blanket? He was a poet. His widow once told me that he loved the nocturnal silence of this building, when there wasn't a soul to be seen. If a poem came to him here, she said, he wouldn't leave until it was finished. At home, in the pretty study furnished by his wife, he felt less at ease. He loved writing here, he didn't mind the bland color of the walls, the dull carpet. The bleakness inspired him. He was an elderly man, a daydreamer, his head whirling with words that found their proper order in this room. He died two years ago. Not here, but he's left something of himself behind. Maybe that's why this room feels a bit sepulchral.

At the Trattoria

I often have lunch at a trattoria close to my house. It's a hole in the wall, so if I don't get there by noon I won't get a seat, and I'll have to wait until after two. I eat alone, next to others eating alone. They're people I don't know, though I frequently encounter a familiar face.

A father cooks, and his daughter waits the tables. I believe the mother died when the daughter was a young girl. This father and daughter share a bond beyond their common blood, one that's been fortified by grief. They're not from around here. Though they work all day on a noisy street, they come from an island. They store the sun's blaze in their bones, barren hills dotted with sheep, the mistral that churns the sea. I picture them together on a boat they've anchored in front of a secluded grotto. I see the daughter diving off the prow, and the father holding a fish that's still breathing in his hands.

Technically the daughter isn't a waitress, given that she's almost always behind the counter.

"What can we get you?"

The menu is handwritten on the blackboard in a compact, whimsical script. I choose a different dish each day of the week. She takes the order and then tells her father, who's always in the kitchen, what to prepare.

When I sit down the daughter brings me a bottle of water, a paper napkin, then resumes her place behind the counter. I wait for my tray to appear, then stand up to retrieve it.

Today, among the tourists and employees who frequent my neighborhood, there's a young father with his daughter. She's around ten years old, with two blond braids, hunched shoulders, a distracted gaze. Normally I see them on Saturdays, but there's no school this week, it's Easter vacation.

By now I know the drill: the daughter refuses to sleep at her father's house, she'll only spend the night with her mother. I used to see them back when they were a family of three, in this very trattoria. I remember when the mother was pregnant with the daughter, and how excited the couple was. I recall how intimately they would speak to one another, and the good wishes expressed by those sitting around them.

They would come to have lunch here even after they became a family. They'd turn up, tired and hungry, after going to the playground, or shopping for food in the piazza. I felt a connection with the little girl, an only child like me, seated between her parents. It's just that my father never liked eating in restaurants.

Last year the mother moved out of our neighborhood, leaving the father behind. And he's frustrated, I'd say exasperated, by the daughter, who remains so loyal to her mother, who refuses to stay at his place, in the house where she was first raised, in the room always awaiting her arrival.

The daughter plays with her cell phone while the father attempts to speak to her, to convince her. I feel sorry listening to him plead. I feel sorry for the parting of ways between this father and daughter, and for the demise of the marriage. Apparently the mother left because he was cheating on her, a passionate affair that's already ended.

"How was school last week?" he asks.

The girl shrugs. "Can you give me a ride to a friend's place tonight?"

"I thought you and I might go to the movies."

"I don't feel like it. I want to go to my friend's."

"What will you do there?"

"I'll have fun."

"And then?"

"I'll go home to Mom's."

The father gives in. He stops trying, this week, to convince her. Now he, too, looks at his cell phone. She only eats part of her dish, and he finishes it for her.

In Spring

In spring I suffer. The season doesn't invigorate me, I find it depleting. The new light disorients, the fulminating nature overwhelms, and the air, dense with pollen, bothers my eyes. To calm my allergies I take a pill in the morning that makes me sleepy. It knocks me out, I can't focus, and by lunchtime I'm tired enough to go to bed. I sweat all day and at night I'm freezing. No shoe seems right for this temperamental time of year.

Every blow in my life took place in spring. Each lasting sting. That's why I'm afflicted by the green of the trees, the first peaches in the market, the light flowing skirts that the women in my neighborhood start to wear. These things only remind me of loss, of betrayal, of disappointment. I dislike waking up and feeling pushed inevitably forward. But today, Saturday, I don't have to leave the house. I can wake up and not have to get up. There's nothing better.

In the Piazza

The daughter of two friends of mine lives alone, like me, in this city. But she's only sixteen. She arrived three years ago with her father, her stepmother, and a stepbrother much younger than she is. The father is a painter and had a big fellowship at an academy up on the hill. I'd met them at one of his exhibits. The painter and his wife used to come to my place for Italian lessons. The daughter never joined them. She attended a high school nearby, and two years later she decided not to return to her country of origin, to separate early from her family and stay on here. She has a room in an apartment the high school oversees, a special residence to house students in her situation.

I call her when there's an exhibit I want to see, or when the sales begin at the end of winter and the start of summer. I'd promised my friends I'd keep an eye on her, even though this girl doesn't need very much from me.

I watch her as she cycles through the piazza. She could be my daughter given that I'm thirty years older. But she's already a woman, with a beauty that's disarming. A girl who smiles as she speaks, as if to declare to the world, See how happy I am. Nothing like I was at that age: still a child, no boyfriends, ill at ease. I'm envious. I still regret my squandered youth, the absence of rebellion.

She's just come back after spending a week with her family. She's relieved to have put some distance between them again. She tells me that spending seven days in a row together is rough: that her father and stepmother are always bickering and that they should separate.

"Don't they love each other?"

"I doubt it. My dad just wants to paint and she's at loose ends, she waits on him hand and foot and it drives him crazy."

"And your mother? Did you see her?"

"She got married again, to a guy I don't like."

She drinks a glass of pomegranate juice. It looks like a glass of blood, though I don't tell her that. She says she's hungry and asks for a cornetto. She splits it in half, then divides one of the pieces. She takes a small bite, then arranges the rest of the pieces on her napkin.

People turn to look at her as we're sitting in the piazza but she doesn't pay them heed. She's fluent in the language her parents struggled to speak. She doesn't look like a tourist or foreigner, she's the type that fits in anywhere.

The parents are worried, they're hoping she'll change her mind and decide to go to a university that's closer to home. I don't tell them, when we speak on the phone, that they've already lost her.

Full of dreams and plans, she believes it's still possible to change the world. She's already brave enough to stand up to authority and she's determined to make a life for herself here. I'm fond of this girl, her grit inspires me. At the same time I think about myself back then and feel depressed. As she tells me about the boys that want to date her, amusing stories that make us both laugh, I can't manage to erase a sense of ineptitude. I feel sad as I laugh; I didn't know love at her age.

What did I do? I read books and studied. I listened to my parents and did what they asked me to. Even though, in the end, I never made them happy. I didn't like myself, and something told me I'd end up alone.

"I talked to your father yesterday, he told me it's raining a lot in your city."

"It's not my city anymore."

"Why don't you like it there?"

"Because I can't stand my stepmother, she has no life, no voice of her own. My mom was basically the same, that's why my dad left her. That dynamic doesn't work anymore. I want to be a strong woman, independent, like you."

I might have said the same thing to her. Instead I say nothing. I watch as she arranges the pieces of uneaten cornetto inside the paper napkin, making a small bundle that she then nestles inside the juice glass. And I ask for the check.

In the Waiting Room

After turning forty-five, after a long and fortunate phase of hardly ever going to the doctor, I grew acquainted with illness. A series of mysterious pains, odd afflictions that would arise out of the blue and then go away: an abiding pressure behind my eyes, a sharp twinge at my elbow, a portion of my face that seemed to have gone numb for a time. Scattered round red spots on my abdomen once generated a stubborn itch so persistent I'd had to go to the emergency room. In the end all it took was an ointment.

For the past few days there's been a strange sensation under the skin at my throat, something along the lines of an irregular palpitation. I only feel it when I'm sitting at home, reading on my couch. That is, when I'm most relaxed, when I'm expecting to feel at peace. It lasts for a few seconds, then passes. When I explained this one morning to my barista—a person I confide all sorts of things to, though I couldn't tell you why—he said:

"I'd get it checked out. There's a vein there that connects your brain to your heart. Take my advice."

And the gentleman standing next to me at the bar, a retired history professor who drinks a glass of beer at the start of each day, added:

"My poor wife, God rest her soul, had complained of something similar."

So I went to the doctor, and after he saw me, after he checked my heartbeat with a shoddy-looking device, he referred me to a cardiologist.

"It's most likely nothing, signora. But given that you're no longer a young girl, it's best to make sure."

And so here I am at this clinic.

The room's a bit dark, the lights are off. The heat feels excessive even though in general I tend to prefer the heat. I start to take off my jacket and scarf right away. There's just one other patient waiting, another woman trapped with me in that room. She looks about twenty years older than I am. She watches me carefully, without warmth in her eyes. Her gaze is impenetrable. I can't manage to remove the scarf, it's gotten tangled up with my necklace. How ridiculous. The woman keeps looking at me as if there were a screen between us, as if I were a person on television.

I unhook the necklace's clasp, feeling rattled, and sit down. I ask:

"How is this doctor? Any good?"

"I wouldn't know."

I wait fifteen minutes, I go on waiting. The other woman also waits. They don't call us in. She doesn't read, she doesn't do anything. She doesn't look at me anymore, not even as if through the television screen.

Unfortunately I forgot to put a book in my purse. There are no magazines. Only a few brochures about health, about taking care of one's heart.

What's this woman's ailment? Is she afraid? I'm tempted to ask her these questions, to break the ice. After all, it's just the two of us. But I know better.

Even though I don't feel any palpitations at the moment, I'm certain that, sooner or later, that vague, worrisome tic will act up again, below my skin, where there's a vein that connects my heart to my brain.

No one keeps this woman company: no caregiver, no friend, no husband. And I bet she knows that in twenty years, when I happen to be in a waiting room like this one for some reason or other, I won't have anyone sitting beside me, either.

In the Bookstore

Inevitably I bump into my ex, the only significant one, with whom I was involved for five years. It's hard to believe, when I see him and say hello, that I ever loved him. He still lives in my neighborhood, alone. He's a small but handsome man, with thin-rimmed eyeglasses and tapered hands that lend him an intellectual air. But he's never amounted to much, he remains puerile and full of complaints, in spite of his middle-aged man's body.

Here he is today in the bookstore. He stops in often, he fancies himself a writer. He was always writing something in a notebook, though I have no idea what. I doubt he's ever managed to publish anything.

"Have you read this?" he asks me, pointing to a book that just got a prize.

"I don't know it."

"You should." He looks at me and adds, "You're looking well."

"You think?"

"I'm a mess, I hardly slept last night."

"Why not?"

"The kids in the bar under my apartment are too rowdy, it's an ongoing problem. I need to find a new place."

"Where?"

"Away from this godforsaken city. I've been thinking of buying a little house by the sea, or maybe in the mountains, far from everything and everyone."

"Are you serious?"

He'll never do it. He's not the type, he's too fearful. When we were together, all I did was listen to him. I would try to solve his problems, even tiny ones. Every time his back went out, every existential crisis. But by now I can look at him without absorbing a drop of that tiresome anxiety, that ongoing lament.

He was terrible at planning or remembering things. Distracted, the opposite of me. He never checked to see what was in the fridge, he'd buy the same stuff twice, we were always tossing food that had gone bad. He was almost always late, there was always some hitch, we were always rushing into the theater halfway through the movie. In the beginning it would irritate me but I got used to it. I adored him, I forgave him.

When we'd go on vacation together he would inevitably forget something essential: shoes for walking, a cream to protect his skin, the notebook for jotting things down. He'd forget to pack the heavy sweater, or the lightweight shirt. He was prone to getting fevers. I've seen several small cities alone while he recovered in a hotel room, while he slept pallid in the bed, coated with sweat under the covers. I made him broth when we got home, I prepared the hot-water bottle, I ran to the pharmacy. I didn't mind playing nurse. Both his parents had died when he was young. You're all I've got in this world, he'd say.

I was happy to cook at his place. I'd spend the entire morning doing the shopping, I'd crisscross the city for the meals I prepared for him. I remember absurd expeditions from one neighborhood to another searching for a particular cheese, for the shiniest eggplants. I'd arrive at his door, I'd set the table, he'd take his place and say: What would I do without your soup, without your roast chicken? Convinced that I was the center of his universe, I took it for granted that, sooner or later, he'd ask me to marry him.

Then one day in April someone rang my buzzer. I thought it was him. Instead it was another woman who knew my boyfriend just as well as I did, who saw him on the days I didn't. I'd shared the same man with this woman for nearly five years. She lived in another neighborhood, and she'd come to know about me thanks to a book I'd lent him, the same book that he, idiotically, in turn, had lent to her. Unbelievable. Inside that book there was a piece of paper, the receipt from a doctor's visit with my name and address. At which point all the little things that had puzzled her about their relationship made sense. She realized that she was only one of his lovers, and that we were an unwitting threesome.

"Did you tell him that you found that receipt? That you were coming to see me?" I asked her once I was able to speak. She was a short woman with bangs, caring eyes, a glow to her skin. She spoke calmly. She had a soothing voice.

"I didn't tell him anything, I didn't see the point. I just wanted to meet you."

"Would you like a coffee?"

We sat down and started to chat. Pulling out our agendas, we reviewed, point by point, details of our parallel relationships: vacations and other memorable moments, herniated disks, bouts of the flu. It was a long and harrowing conversation. A meticulous exchange of information, of disparate dates that solved a mystery, that dispelled a nightmare I'd been unconsciously living. We realized that we were two survivors, and in the end we felt like partners in a crime. Each revelation was devastating. Everything she said. And yet, even as my life shattered in pieces, I felt as if I were finally coming up for air. The sun started to set and we were hungry, and when there was nothing left to say we went out to share a meal.

In My Head

Solitude: it's become my trade. As it requires a certain discipline, it's a condition I try to perfect. And yet it plagues me, it weighs on me in spite of my knowing it so well. It's probably my mother's influence. She's always been afraid of being alone and now her life as an old woman torments her, so much that when I call to ask how she's doing, she just says, I'm very alone. She says she misses having amusing and surprising experiences, this even though she has lots of friends who love her, and a social life far more complicated and lively than mine. The last time I went to visit her, for example, the phone kept ringing. And yet she's always on edge, I'm not sure why. She's burdened by the passage of time.

When I was young, even when my father was alive, she kept me close to her side, she never wanted us to be apart, not even briefly. She safeguarded me, she protected me from solitude as if it were a nightmare, or a wasp. We were an unhealthy amalgam until I left to lead a life of my own. Was I the shield between her and her terror, was I the one who kept her from sinking into the abyss? Was it the fear of her fear that's led me to a life like this?

For years we've both been alone and I know that deep down she'd like to reconstruct that amalgam, thereby extinguishing our mutual solitude. In her opinion it would solve both our problems. But since I don't give in, since I refuse to live in the same city, I prolong her suffering. If I tell my mother that I'm grateful to be on my own, to be in charge of my space and my time—this in spite of the silence, in spite of the lights I never switch off when I leave the house, along with the radio I always keep playing—she'd look at me, unconvinced. She'd say solitude was a lack and nothing more. There's no point discussing it given that she's blind to the small pleasures my solitude affords me. In spite of how she's clung to me over the years my point of view doesn't interest her, and this gulf between us has taught me what solitude really means.

At the Museum

Even though it's right next to the train station, in the midst of perpetual crowds, my favorite museum is almost always empty. I like to stop by in the late afternoon, after work; I recognize the guards who spend all day on folding chairs, chatting among themselves in front of mosaics, friezes, frescoes, tiled floors.

The museum features a number of houses from antiquity. They were excavated, pried from their surroundings, removed, relocated, displayed to the public. They've reconstructed a few bedrooms, with walls painted red, or a dark hue of yellow, or black, or sky blue. Rooms in which, centuries ago, people slept, dreamt, were bored, made love.

The most beautiful room—it belonged to an emperor's consort—has a garden painted onto the walls, teeming with trees, flowers, citrus plants, animals. Pomegranates have split open and birds perch on the branches of the trees. The scene is fixed, faded. The trees, with their thin branches, seem to bend as if from the soft breeze that courses through the landscape. This semblance of a breeze is what makes the painted nature tremble, rendering everything paradoxically alive.

In the middle of this room there are two soft benches covered in black leather. I sit down to observe the sun. It penetrates the glass roof and filters the light, causing the tonalities of the trees and shrubs in the fresco to change. The shifting light brightens and darkens the room in turns. It's a panorama that makes me think of the sea, of swimming in a clear blue patch underwater.

Today an elegant woman about my age walks into the room. She looks like a foreigner. I bet she's in the city by chance, maybe tagging along behind her husband, who's here for work and busy all day. She has a resigned air, and she looks a bit put out. She's obligated to be a tourist.

She knows nothing about this room and doesn't seem particularly impressed. Maybe she's thinking, as she sits in this stunning space, about how much she's had to walk today, and how tired she is. Maybe she's thinking of her house in some other part of the world. She's already missing that ordinary dwelling. She's seen her share of churches and fountains and by now she's saturated. She's got a tiny hotel room, it's either too hot or too cold. She sleeps poorly due to jet lag.

She sits down on the comfortable bench. She's sick of setting out each day and studying the map of the city to find the roads she needs to follow. After taking in the four walls of the room she looks away, lowers her head, looks down. She studies her swollen feet, her shoes, and thinks about all the streets she's walked in the past few days, in a vast city, alone, disoriented all the while. She's not moved by the beauty of this room. She takes advantage of it to restore her energy.

She closes her eyes and stretches out on the bench without paying any attention to me. She lies down on her back, her eyes closed. That's how she manages to fully inhabit and possess this room, crossing a certain threshold I've always respected.

On the Couch

I saw a therapist for about a year. She lived in a far-flung neighborhood I didn't know well. The building was pink, built long ago. There was a sarcophagus in the courtyard, lots of plants, a few amphoras. The elevator was made of wood and glass, with slender double doors that led to a tiny compartment. The apartment was also cozy, always partly shaded, the shutters partly closed. The couch for patients, plum-colored, was right there where you entered. The room was so small that it felt like a beautifully furnished closet, but the ceiling was high and books covered the walls from top to bottom. Maybe I chose that therapist simply because I loved arriving in that courtyard, riding up in that elevator, entering that room.

I would lie back on the couch and she sat in an armchair behind me, looking at me. Or maybe she looked somewhere else. She was an attractive woman with dark eyes and a space between her front teeth. Behind a set of doors was the life she led with the rest of her family: the pantry full of food, dirty dishes to wash, the laundry drying on a rack. All I knew was the space dedicated to curing her patients: an individual sanatorium that hosted one anguished soul at a time.

She always started by saying the same thing: Please begin. As if each session were the first and only time we met. Every session was like the start of a novel abandoned after the first chapter.

What did I talk to her about? Dreams, nightmares, nonsense. Sometimes I'd recount my mother's fitful rages, the quarrels I've never forgotten, terrifying scenes my mother no longer has any memory of. I'd talk about all the ways my mother found fault with me. How severely she'd berate me. The oppressive mother who weighs nothing today, the invasive mother who, in her old age, struggles to take a step. The father who died suddenly when I was fifteen.

"I've been having nightmares," I mentioned one day.

"About what?"

"A square container of glass, enormous, full of my blood."

"How did you know it was your blood?"

"I can't remember. But I knew it was mine."

"Anything else?"

"A few days ago I had a dream about my bed. It was full of black bugs, they were crawling all over the sheets."

"Were you sleeping among them?"

"Yes, but when I realized it I got out of bed, I was horrified. Then when I looked at them closely I saw that they were sweet-looking, with kind eyes that seemed almost human, and that reassured me."

"So the dream about the blood in the glass container was more upsetting?"

"I'd say so, yes."

At every session she would ask me to tell her something positive. Unfortunately my childhood harbors few happy memories. Instead I would tell her about the balcony off my apartment when the sun is shining and I'm having breakfast. And I would tell her how much I like to sit outside, pick up a warm pen in my hand, and write down a sentence or two.

On the Balcony

I, too, act as a therapist for a friend of mine. She's in her forties like me but she's rushing through life, she's always harried. She has everything I don't: a husband, kids, constant plans, a country house. In other words, the successful life my parents had hoped I'd lead one day. My friend works hard, she's got an important job that sends her around the world. This means she's off to the airport at least once a month, leaving her family behind. Her suitcase is always packed and ready, with pills to calm her down, given that she hates flying. She's racked with guilt but she doesn't let up, she's always on the move.

She comes over now and then. Something tells me my spartan place is a refuge for her. I make her a cup of tea. "This is the only place where I can relax," she says. She likes the silence, and not seeing objects scattered everywhere. She likes my glass coffee table and the piles of books arranged on it, a few stones I've picked up along the seashore.

She says: "In my house I can never just sit and be. There's always something that needs to be done, I never lean back on the sofa and check out for a minute. The coffee table is always a mess, it depresses me to look at it. In that house I'm only happy when I'm sleeping. But, God, we spent a fortune fixing it up. I think in the end all I need is a little corner to myself. I'd love a tiny apartment like yours."

Before she was married she used to live like I do. She describes the place: the small living room, the bedroom that looked over the courtyard, the morning light that flickered on the carpet. She didn't mind the noisy street, the old pipes and heating. One day she confessed that, in spite of her fear of planes, she loves the nook she occupies in flight, the seat that becomes her bed, the lamp behind her shoulder, everything she needs at arm's reach.

Today she's distraught and she smokes a cigarette. We're sitting on the balcony, where there's space for two metal chairs. She tells me that she's just gotten back from a long trip overseas, and discovered a notebook belonging to her younger daughter. It contains a story about a girl who misses her mother, who feels abandoned. It begins: "There was a little girl who always felt lonely, who cried every night before going to bed because her mother was almost never there to wish her good night."

She shows me the notebook. The story is hand-written, illustrated with neatly drawn pictures. The mother, with short dark hair, resembles my friend. She wears a scarf around her neck, lipstick, and holds a suitcase in her hand. There's a taxi in the background waiting to take her away.

"Can you keep this for me?" she asks.

"Why?"

"Because it was written for me, it's mine, I should keep it and I don't want to lose it. But my house is a mess and I can never find anything there, I can't even get my own bearings, and also . . ."

"Also?"

"I don't want my husband to come across it."

I set aside the notebook. "I'll look after it," I say.

"Will you stay put for a while?" I ask.

"I leave again next week. It's an insane stretch. I'm hoping things will slow down this summer."

But then she starts talking about her husband's family, and the vacation she has to take with them in August to celebrate an important anniversary of her in-laws. "I wish I didn't have to go, after three days with them I start to lose it."

I almost ask: Isn't that the case with your husband and kids, with your house? Isn't that why you're always traveling, why you leave them behind every other week?

I don't say this. I'm fond of my friend, I let her blow off steam. The sun beats down on us and chafes the skin below my sweater.

In the Pool

Twice a week, at dinnertime, I go to the pool. In that container of clear water lacking life or current I see the same people with whom, for whatever reason, I feel a connection. We see each other without ever planning to. They come at the same time, on those same days, to escape life's troubles.

Here's the elderly woman who walks with a limp, leaning on a cane. The space is like an amphitheater and it's hard for her to make it from the locker room to the edge of the pool. She uses the ladder to get in and always swims with her face above water. Next to her is the guy with the shaved head who dives deep and does laps for over an hour, never stopping. His potent somersaults send him down nearly half a length before he comes up again for air. It's an enormous pool and the eight lanes are almost always occupied. Eight different lives share that water at a time, never intersecting.

I swim for about forty minutes, maybe fifty, before I get tired. I'm not a strong swimmer, I can't do a flip turn, I never learned how. The idea of being on my back underwater scares me a little. I typically do the crawl, with a weak but decent stroke.

In the pool I lose myself. My thoughts merge and flow. Everything—my body, my heart, the universe—seems tolerable when I'm protected by water and nothing touches me. All I think about is the effort. Below my body there's a restless play of dark and light projected onto the bottom of the pool, that drifts away like smoke. I'm surrounded by an element that restores me, one in which my mother wouldn't know how to survive.

She was the one who brought me to the pool when I was little. She'd wait for me, she'd watch me from above, seated on the bleachers, always slightly nervous as I learned to float and breathe and kick. Water can cover me without drowning me. My mother and I are different that way. Perhaps a few drops enter my nose or ears, but my body resists. And yet, every time I swim, I feel cleansed as if from within.

It's just that in the locker room, when the other women chat among themselves, I'm prey to terrible stories, brutal information shared as they take their showers, take off their swimsuits, shave their legs and armpits and groins in awkward, contorted poses.

That's how one day a young mother, responding to a woman who remarked, "I haven't seen you here lately," talked about her son's cancer, a little boy, just eighteen months old. He's already had two operations. She recounted trips to the best hospitals, the hellish treatment, the precarious recovery.

A few days later two women discussed the adult son of a third woman they both knew. He'd had an accident while on vacation with his family; he'd slipped in such a way that now he was paralyzed, and risked never walking again.

"God, what a nightmare," one of the women said before turning on the hair dryer and grooming herself.

Today a woman in her eighties who swims four days a week shares a memory that surprises us: she admits that she's afraid of the sea, because of a huge wave that once knocked her down and twisted her up when she was a girl.

"I was about to drown," she says, still stunned. "When I was tossed onto the shore, water was pouring out of my nose, my mouth, my ears. My arms were scraped from top to bottom."

She'd been swimming with an aunt who, seeing her frightened, had held her hand, but that human anchor had only caused more harm. She'd have been better off nearly drowning on her own.

It's hard to imagine her body when it was young. Over the years it's lost its shape, she's hunched over, covered with moles. She gets dressed, combs her hair, and puts on a few gold rings, including her wedding band.

In this humid, rusty place where women congregate, naked and wet, where they show each other the scars beside their breasts and on their bellies, the bruises on their thighs, the imperfections on their backs, they all talk about misfortune. They complain about husbands, children, aging parents. They confess things without feeling guilty.

As I take in these losses, these tragedies, it occurs to me that the water in the pool isn't so clear after all. It reeks of grief, of heartache. It's contaminated. And after I get out I'm saturated by a vague sense of dread. All that suffering doesn't leak out like the water that travels into my ear now and then. It burrows into my soul, it wedges itself into every nook of my body.

The old woman closes her purse and politely says goodbye, but before leaving, as I'm drying my limbs, she says,

"I've got a bunch of dresses in my closet that would look good on you. They're adorable but I can't wear them anymore. Would you like them, so they don't go to waste?" She adds, without skipping a beat, "It's been decades since I've had a waist."

On the Street

I spot them on the street, in the middle of a crowd
of pedestrians waiting for the light to change:
the couple who live around the corner, my friend
and the kind man I cross paths with now and again
on the bridge. I quicken my pace to catch up to them,
I think of saying hello, but then I realize that they're
having an argument. It's a wide avenue, there's confusion right and left. You can hardly hear a thing but
they manage to make themselves heard. They talk at
the same time, their sentences overlapping so that it's
impossible to know what they're fighting about. Then
I hear her voice: "Don't touch me, you disgust me."

I start to follow them. I don't go into the store I was
heading to, it's not urgent. We cross the broad street
together. He's handsome, lanky. She's got long hair, a
bit tousled, and wears a flame-colored, egg-shaped
coat.

They pay no attention to passersby, they're not

ashamed of fighting in public. It's as if they're in the middle of nowhere, on a deserted beach, or inside a home. They're having a bad, bitter fight. It rises above the mayhem that surrounds them; they act as if they're the only people who inhabit the entire city.

She's furious, and in the beginning he tries to appease her. But then he, too, loses his temper, and he's as irritated and spiteful as she is. It feels unseemly, a quarrel so intimate in front of everyone. Their biting words pierce the air as if physically puncturing it, seeping into the blue of the sky, blackening it. And it upsets me to notice that his face has turned mean.

At the intersection she says, "See those two?"

She points to an elderly couple. They hold hands and walk with measured steps, in silence.

"I wanted us to get where they've gotten."

My friends aren't so young anymore, either, even though they're now behaving like children. After crossing the busy avenue, we turn onto a quieter street. I'm still walking a few paces behind them. And as I do I begin to understand what they're arguing about.

They'd gone to their daughter's school to listen to a concert and then they'd stopped to have a coffee. After that she wanted to take a taxi home, whereas he wanted to walk. He'd offered to call her a taxi and then return on foot. And this suggestion had offended her to the point where she'd exploded.

Now she's saying that he'd never have suggested such a thing when they were first dating, when he was deeply in love with her.

"It's a bad sign," she says.

He replies drily, "You're out of your mind, you don't know what you're saying."

"You're always going your own way these days. I don't see how we can resolve this."

After making this statement, she starts to cry. But he keeps walking slightly ahead of her. At the next intersection he stops and she catches up to him.

"Why were you so opposed to walking and enjoying this sunny day?"

"I'm wearing a new pair of shoes that I haven't broken in yet."

"Well, you could have told me that."

"You could have asked."

At that point I stop following them, having already heard too much.

At the Beautician

I n general I avoid spa treatments. I'm not too keen on the idea of lying in a little room wearing a blindfold with mud spread over my body. I wear my hair long, there's only a bit of gray, so all I need is a good cut one afternoon at the hairdresser's, once a season. I wax my legs at home while I watch something trashy on TV. My one indulgence, twice a month, always on a Sunday, is getting my nails done, and this forces me, at least for an hour, to not do anything at all. No phone calls to make, no text messages to send, no newspapers to read or glossy magazines to leaf through.

I sit in front of a woman, rarely the same one. The beauticians also sit in a row, like the clients, behind a long narrow counter. There's a mirror, just as long, that doubles the whole scene and all the work that takes place. I wonder how dull it is for them, while we clients relax. All the women come from the same country, and while they diligently see to our needs they talk continuously in their language. I always wonder what they're talking about.

Lately there's a stunning young woman among them. The others look tired, most of them are heavy-set, round-faced, their lips misshapen. But this one's a beauty: elegant, her dark hair drawn back and parted down the middle, her cheekbones prominent. The cotton apron that the rest of them wear looks like a dress sewn to fit her body. I feel more like the others, disheveled. I glance over at her now and then, her beauty distracts me, her features are so perfect. After I look at her I look at myself in the mirror, and yet again I resign myself to the fact that my face has always disappointed me. Every look in the mirror dismays me, that's the reason I tend to avoid them.

Today I'm in a rush, I walk in without an appointment. I just need the polish taken off. The week before, feeling blue, I chose a dark vampy shade, but two days later it already started to chip.

"Hello, signora. Would you like a manicure?" the manager of the salon asks me.

"I don't have time today, how much is it to remove the color?"

"Oh there's no charge for that. Not for you. Just a tip for the girl."

So I sit down in front of the beautiful one. She's serious, she welcomes me without smiling, and she starts to study my nails immediately, as if they were her own.

She's not hasty like the others. I give her my hands, she takes them into her own, and for a while she and I are connected. She smiles and speaks to the other women seated beside her without ever raising her head. She enjoys herself, all the while focused on her task. She takes off the polish, I'm sorry she's already finished.

"Listen, I've changed my mind. Can you put some new color on, please?"

"Of course."

She proceeds to work on my nails. She delicately eliminates the skin that grows around them. I see the little pile that accumulates, lifeless shards of myself. Satisfied, she applies a thick white cream and wraps my hands in a hot steaming towel. I don't look at myself in the mirror while she perfects this one part of my body. I don't want to spoil the moment, or this contact between us. I'd like to appreciate her attention and nothing else, so I try to focus exclusively on her, acknowledging that though we're united we're two separate people. For about twenty minutes this woman sitting between me and the mirror protects me from my reflection, from the image that haunts me, and as a result, at least this time, I feel beautiful, too.

She has a deep voice, and that language, coming from her throat, doesn't sound harsh to my ears. At one point she stops to admire one of my rings.

"Husband?"

"I'm not married."

She laughs. She doesn't say anything else. She has nice white teeth. Why did she laugh? I don't trust that laugh, it disconcerts me. The last thing she does is apply a pink polish, nearly transparent. My nails look good, but hers, untouched, uncolored, are lovelier still.

In the Hotel

I need to spend three nights out of town for a convention. The hotel is full, besieged by my colleagues. I dread this annual event: the same convention, the same crowd. The only thing that changes is the city in which it's held, and therefore, the hotel.

This year, as soon as I set foot inside, I'm compelled to turn around and leave. The entrance, with its massive lobby, swallows me up. I'm nothing beneath that high ceiling. It's an ugly hotel, noisy and cavernous. The space looks like a parking garage designed for human beings instead of cars, with curved balconies that rise up and up. They're all built around an atrium, a chasm with places to drink and buy expensive scarves, shoes, and bags.

There are other groups all around, mostly men dressed in gray, herds of them, all of them laughing too loudly, too often. Their laughter reverberates and fills up the chasm, ringing out again and again.

My room, thank goodness, doesn't face this collective chasm. The staff person tells me that in order to reach it I need to walk quite a ways, then proceed down a long hallway that leads to an elevator. It takes me five minutes just to get there.

The room is crammed with objects: drinking glasses, bottles of water, a kettle, mugs, tea bags, ugly leather folders, magazines, information about the hotel and about the city written on various pieces of folded paper. There's not an empty surface, no place to set anything down. I can't locate my own things in this confusion. At least the closet, apart from the iron and the white bathrobe, is empty. I open my suitcase and hang up a few dresses.

I just want to get to the other side of these three days, these three awful nights. During the days I'll be busy, in some conference room or another listening to speeches and panels. I'll just follow the schedule. At night, on the other hand, I already know that I'm not going to get any sleep in this room they've stuck me in. It's the kind of room that makes me hate the world. I'd toss all this stuff out the window, if I could. I might even toss myself out. I'm on the twelfth floor. But these windows don't open.

The only consolation during the next few days is a gentleman who occupies the room next door. He's a scholar of some sort: circumspect, detached from his surroundings, absorbed by something else. He's thin with a head full of curly white hair. He strikes me as a man at peace with himself but at odds with the world, the type that dwells on things too much. But his large eyes are tender, tinged with sadness.

When he sees me he smiles instead of saying hello. He looks at me kindly, never crossing the line, while we wait for the elevator and wait to face the day together. But his watchful gaze seems to say, Signora, I know you're having a hard time. He doesn't try to cheer me up, he just conveys a certain understanding.

I'm curious about him, enough to leaf through the conference brochure to learn his name. He's a well-known philosopher who has written several books, a refugee from a country whose brutal regime persecuted him many years ago. I wish I could have gone to his event but I can't get out of attending my own. Something tells me that the quiet philosopher is really a lively soul, and that hidden beneath that shy exterior is a man who appreciates a good joke.

What does he think of me? A middle-aged woman, slightly on edge, annoyed to find herself at an academic conference?

In the evenings we ride up together in the elevator and he says good night, always courteously but sincerely, always looking me in the eye and then saluting me with a nod of his head before opening the door to his room. I hear his footsteps while he gets undressed and relaxes after a hectic day, while he brushes his teeth. I picture him as he throws himself onto a bed identical to mine, in a room just as hideous. It's only at this time of night that he reveals another aspect of himself: he has long talks on the telephone, speaking rapidly and heatedly in another language. With whom? His wife? A friend? His publisher? His company reassures me though he doesn't interest me sexually, it's not about that. I think of the melancholy in his eyes, that wanting look. Eyes, bright but distant, that are about to close for six or seven hours.

The next day we open our doors and exit at the same time, riding down in the elevator together before going our separate ways. Without planning to, we wait for each other every morning and every evening, and for three days our tacit bond puts me obscurely at peace with the world.

At the Ticket Counter

One rainy afternoon I walk down a long street lined with shops. I pass groups of people who've decided to loiter at the storefronts for a few minutes: families, husbands and wives, teenage couples, tourists. I see some elegant women who behave as if they've been friends for decades and are having fun in spite of the rain. They succumb to a few pastries even though they're always on a diet, and they take advantage of the sales. Years ago this used to be a stylish commercial street, but now cheap chain stores have taken it over, the same ones found in airports all over the world.

I feel like the only one with a specific goal this afternoon. I keep walking under my large, taut umbrella. There's no wind.

At the end of the street there's a magnificent theater built in the 1800s: one of the few remaining jewels in this run-down city. There's no one waiting in line at the box office. I ask for the program, newly printed, for the next season, and I'm given a thin booklet with smooth pages. Instead of returning home to read it at my leisure I stand there in front of the ticket window. I read about the shows coming in autumn, in winter. The young person behind the window lets me study things at my own pace.

I take out a pen and mark a series of operas, symphonies, and dance performances I'd like to see. I recognize a few of the actors and musicians. I study the map of the theater, the arrangement of the seats in relation to the stage. I don't have a fixed spot. I like to choose a different one each time and enjoy the concerts and performances from various points of view. I peruse all the options and feel drawn to certain shows both before and after dinner. That way, I'll vary the routine. I know that the tickets, once purchased, are not refundable. Buying them is always a gamble, a leap of faith. It makes me anxious, and also makes me feel intrepid.

This is how I fill up the pages of my agenda, the one I buy at the end of every year at the same stationery store, always the same size and number of pages. Little notebooks in various colors that, with the passing of years, inevitably repeat: blue, red, black, brown, red, blue, black, and so on. A set of matching editions that sum up my life.

I make a list of the performances I'd like to attend.

"Just one ticket?" the person behind the window asks.

"Just one."

But how will I be feeling at eight-thirty at night on May 16 next year? There's no way of knowing. I proceed with the hope that I'll be back, with the ticket in hand, wearing a nice dress, occupying a comfortable seat.

It was my father, who worked behind the window of a post office, who introduced me to the theater. He loved this world. My mother never went.

One time he'd booked tickets for a play running in a city just across the border. He'd wanted to take me, he'd wanted to treat me, early, for one of my birthdays.

"It's bad luck to celebrate a birthday before it comes," my mother said. But on the day of my birthday—I was turning fifteen—the show would have already ended. So we booked the train, packed our suitcases, and organized our passports.

The night before leaving, my father didn't feel well. He came down with a high fever. It looked like he had the flu but he couldn't lift his head from the pillow. He was admitted to the hospital for a few days. Bacteria had entered his bloodstream, and in the end, instead of going to see a play with him, I sat at his wake. The long train trip and the hotel and the actors onstage were replaced by the pageant of mourning. At the funeral one of my aunts, a little drunk, said: "There's no escaping the unforeseen. We live day by day."

I pay in cash and the person behind the window hands me my change. A coin falls, but it doesn't hit the ground. It's ended up inside my umbrella. The umbrella's deep, also wet. I don't want to stick my arm down there and search among the ribs.

There's a group of elderly people behind me now. They want to visit the theater, there's a guided tour in fifteen minutes. I've always found those tours silly, but it's pouring outside, so I, too, ask for a ticket. It's a minor expense. I join the group and for the first time I learn the history of the place that reminds me of my father. The guide talks to us about the shape of the theater, the style of the curtains, the fact that there's a huge void above the lovely fresco on the ceiling. He tells us the name of the king who commissioned the structure two centuries ago, and the date of the fire that destroyed an entire section.

The people I'm with admire the theater as if it were a famous cathedral. They ask questions: Where were

the original plans kept? After the fire, did they reconstruct it in the same style? There are quite a few of us
because of the rain. The stage, expansive and messy,
is in the midst of being set up for something. A few
workmen are hammering nails into the floor.

We gather in the royal box, the highlight of the tour.
How depressing. I feel trapped with all those tourists,
what was I thinking? A few people strike poses in the
royal box. Once it was an exclusive space, off-limits
to people like us. But now, as long as we pay a little
money, we're welcome to enjoy it for a few minutes.
A man takes a picture of his wife, as if she were the
queen. I try to step out of the way but we're crammed
together, it's too late. I'm caught in the charade, I play
a part in it, albeit as an extra.

In the Sun

Today there are protests downtown, and the helicopters have been circling the city all morning. But it's the sun that wakes me up, and it beckons me to my desk, where I write, wrapped in my robe, and then it draws me down to the piazza, where I'm greeted by the contained mayhem of my neighborhood.

It's a splendid Saturday, the first warm day. Only a few people are still wearing boots, I see parkas unzipped and the blistered heels of girls in flip-flops who can't stand their punishing leather ballerina flats anymore. Even though it's Saturday there's still a dash of elegance to how people are dressed: the bold shade of a jacket, a bright scarf, the tight lines of a dress. It feels like a party effortlessly organized at the last minute. The piazza becomes a beach on days like this, and a sense of well-being, of euphoria, permeates the air. All the stores are full of people, long lines at the bank machine, the butcher, the bakery, but no one's complaining. If anything they enjoy the wait. While I'm in line for a sandwich a woman says, "What a spectacular day." And the man behind her says, "This neighborhood is always spectacular."

It's my turn for the sandwich.

"Just wait and see how delicious this one's going to be," the man behind the counter says. He's known me forever and makes me the same sandwich at least three times a week. "Today it's going to be the best ever."

He dips a ladle into a bucket on the counter. He weighs two slices of fresh cheese on the scale, arranges them on a roll, wraps the sandwich in paper, and gives me the bill. "Here you go, my dear."

It hardly costs anything. I look for a place to sit and find a spot in the playground where they deal drugs at night, but at this time of day it's bursting with kids, parents, dogs, also a few people on their own like me. But today I don't feel even slightly alone. I hear the babble of people as they chatter, on and on. I'm amazed at our impulse to express ourselves, explain ourselves, tell stories to one another. The simple sandwich I always get amazes me, too. As I eat it, as my body bakes in the sun that pours down on my neighborhood, each bite, feeling sacred, reminds me that I'm not forsaken.

At My House

An old friend comes to visit; we haven't seen each other in ages. I've known her since I was a child. We went to the same school, then the same high school in the center, then the same university, but after that she went to live abroad and doesn't return too often. She got married a few years ago, after a long period of living on her own. She had a daughter. She got in touch recently, saying she'd be back for a week of vacation. She'd like me to meet her family.

They come by for tea. I've placed a tray on the dining table with pastries I went out to buy this morning. The little girl is two years old. She goes into the living area and amuses herself quietly while the adults have their tea. My friend sets her up on the couch, handing her some books and toys, saying, "Don't touch anything, my love."

The husband, a skinny guy who looks a few years

younger than she is, talks about their busy schedule. Museum exhibits and monuments they want to see, people to meet up with.

"My wife was heart-set on fitting in time to visit you," he tells me.

He's an academic who writes books. It's easy to see him standing at the lectern, even though, to tell the truth, he feels more like one of my precocious students. He mentions that his father was a diplomat and that he was raised all over the world. He strikes me as a pompous man. He's not even attractive. His eyes are small and his lips look tight. The city doesn't enchant him, after just two days he's complaining about our haphazard way of life. He says, "The amount of garbage is insane. The streets are complete chaos. How do people live here?" And I wonder, what exactly did he learn about the world after living in all those different countries?

He eats almost all the pastries I'd bought with the little girl in mind. The child prefers dry, tasteless biscuits transported from abroad, stored in her knapsack. "We always keep a packet in there, that way she feels at home wherever we go," my friend explains.

The husband selects the creamiest, stickiest pastries, the ones with jam on the inside or chocolate on the outside. "We're skipping dinner tonight and taking a long walk, instead. I need to work off all this heavy food."

Maybe he doesn't like me, either. He probably can't figure out why his wife, who's such a sweet and cheerful woman, ever became friends with someone moody like me. Not quite what you made her out to be, he'll remark later on. What was she like when you knew her? he'll ask. But I, on my end, also feel sorry for my friend for marrying such an ill-mannered man. On the other hand, they've produced a well-behaved child.

Out of the blue he gets up and starts studying my bookshelves, scrutinizing all my books. What he's really doing is studying me. I don't like the way he's looking at those books, it gets on my nerves. He pulls one out and opens it, he reads a bit while his wife takes the little girl to the bathroom. It's a book of poems, an out-of-print volume that I'd picked up one Sunday at a flea market. I'd haggled long and hard on the price.

"Any good?"

"I think so, yes."

"I tried to read him years ago and I quit after two pages, I couldn't get through it."

"I like him. I think he's a great writer."

"Can I borrow this?"

It comes out more as a statement than a question. And without hesitating I reply: "I'm sorry, but you're traveling, who knows when we'll see each other again?"

He glances at me, dismissive, but doesn't say anything else. He returns the book to its place. I feel stingy but I can't lend my book to this man, I just can't.

My friend comes back and I notice that her green eyes, once full of light, have dulled slightly. We talk about other things. Then, somewhat abruptly, they say they have to go, they have another appointment.

I say goodbye. I wish I could have seen my friend without her husband in tow. He had done most of the talking.

"Let's stay in touch," she says, already at the elevator, holding her daughter in her arms. "Should we get together, just you and me?"

"Whenever you'd like," I tell her. But I know they'll be too busy, and that this won't happen.

I tidy up the house and put the remaining pastries in a tin so that I can savor them slowly at breakfast for the rest of the week. Then I go check on the book he'd wanted to take away. I hope the cover hasn't been stained by jam or chocolate. Thank goodness he hasn't left a trace. No doubt he thought: This woman owns thousands of books and yet she's unwilling to lend me even one. But I treasure this volume, and I doubt that he'd be able to appreciate a single word of it.

I return to the living room and am about to sit where the little girl had been playing when I see that she's drawn a thin errant line on the white leather covering the back of the couch, with the ballpoint pen I'd left on the coffee table, next to a pile of books.

He'd been the one to put her toys into the knapsack again. No doubt he'd noticed the couch, the back of it, and the line that hadn't been there before. But he'd said nothing to the little girl, nothing to me. He'd given me a kiss and said goodbye, thanking me for the tea.

The line is like a long strand of hair, innocuous, intolerable. A line that drifts and drifts. I can't rub it away with my finger. Nothing I do to try to lift it works. I buy cushions, a blanket to hide it. But they're not a solution, the cushions move around and the blanket slips down. I read on the armchair now.

In August

In August my neighborhood thins out: it wastes away like an old woman who was once a stunning beauty before shutting down completely. Some people spend the month here on purpose; they hole up gladly, turning antisocial. Others cower at the thought of those shapeless days and weeks, the severe closure. Their moods dip, they flee. I'm not a great fan of this month, but I don't hate it, either.

At first I enjoy the peace and quiet. I greet the neighbors who are still around, who walk out in their flip-flops as if they were in some sleepy seaside town. In the few stores that remain open, at the coffee bar, people talk about their plans, upcoming vacations. They say: I love parking wherever I want, these days there's so little traffic you can cross the avenue with your eyes closed. It's startling to see the piazza nearly abandoned. Then at a certain point everything grows static, choked by silence and inertia, and the very lack of activity feels, paradoxically, depleting.

For the past few days the bars have been shut tight, I can't even have a coffee outside my home. I go out in the late morning anyway, to buy food: only two of the farm stands are open, there's not much. The food looks flaccid. It's overpriced and already half-cooked by the sun. The proprietors stand like statues under their white tents: mute, listless characters in a mise-en-scène. They're not the people I like to buy from. The ones I'm loyal to, who give me a discount, are away. These two are wily, they're cheating the tourists who come here for a week or two, who rent the apartments of people who normally live on the piazza and are spending these weeks on their boats, or in the mountains, or abroad. The tourists visit the city in spite of the torrid heat, the gloomy atmosphere.

It's impossible to spend money other than at the market. All the store owners are on vacation, they've pulled down their grates not for a death in the family but for merriment, and they've left exuberant hand-written signs with exclamation marks on their doors wishing everyone a good vacation and saying when they'll open up again. But this year there's something unusual going on: one of my neighbors—he's a guy in his thirties, a bit unkempt—has decided to get rid of certain things in his house. He lives in an atypical building, it looks as though it was originally a storefront. It has a grate instead of windows or a front door.

He sits for half the day in a pair of shorts—I bet he also sleeps in them—on a stool in the middle of the alleyway closed to traffic. It's a road to park on, or to turn down simply in order to back out again. Next to the stool, he's set up two or three folding tables, and on them he displays a series of objects that are both useful and utterly useless: vases, silverware, science textbooks, chipped hand-painted porcelain bowls, lackluster teacups, toys, various knickknacks. Women's shoes, pretty but battered. Evening bags lined with silk that's faded and slightly soiled. There's an ugly multicolored fur on a hanger, out of place, totally out of season.

He's arranged books in a lopsided hutch that belongs in a kitchen. The costume jewelry sits on one of the tables, on top of a piece of velvet. Plates and bowls are carefully stacked on the same table. I ask myself: How many meals behind those beaten-up forks and knives? How many bouquets of fresh flowers filled those vases before withering? Every day the merchandise changes slightly as he combs through more layers of stuff. *Cheap Deals* he's written on a piece of paper. When I ask how much something costs, he almost always tells me the same price.

In the afternoon, before lunch, he moves all his objects inside, pulls down the grate, and goes somewhere, probably to the beach. The following morning, he's there again. As I pass by his house I catch a glimpse of the dark, dusty, jumbled source of his little venture.

I say hi to him every day, I pause to look at this and that. I worry that it would seem impolite not to. At the same time, even though he's the one putting everything on display, I feel hesitant, somehow invasive. I worry about touching his things, I feel strange coveting them, wanting to purchase them.

A painting on canvas, not too big, catches my eye. It's a portrait of a girl with short, side-parted hair. The portrait is unfinished. There are no shoulders, no bust, instead there's just the dirty surface of the canvas. The girl seems anxious, she gives me a sidelong glance.

My neighbor—is he the hale and hearty son of the pallid young girl?—is friendly, but he doesn't pester me. He's rather indifferent to my curiosity. In any case, since all the stores are closed, I decide to give him some business. One day I buy a couple of drinking glasses. Then, for the same price, I buy a magazine that was sold thirty-three years ago at a newsstand, that was read, perhaps, on a train. I buy a necklace. Then I buy the portrait. The more I buy, the more new things turn up on the tables. In the stark summer desert, this oasis of objects, this ongoing flow of goods, reminds me that everything vanishes, and also reminds me of the banal, stubborn residue of life.

Even though I don't need any of this stuff, I keep buying things from him. And back at my house, in the mornings, I taste the day's first coffee from one of those chipped cups. I read the magazine on my balcony and learn all about the actors and gossip and goings-on of another generation. I hang up the portrait and look at that young, timid face. What would have made her happy? Did she grow up to wear that flashy fur coat? Was it hers? Did she like feeling elegant, being admired as she rushed about doing errands in winter under a chilly blue sky?

One day the young man invites me in, he owes me some change. As soon as I set foot in the room I'm uneasy. The life lived in that house overwhelms me. It's all been hoarded, neglected, ransacked.

Finally I ask, "Who owned these things?"

"My family. And me. I put together all those puzzles. I graduated from high school because I read those books. My mother cooked meals for decades in those pots and pans. My dad played with those cards. He never tossed anything out. When she died he didn't want to get rid of her things. But this year he died, too, so it's up to me, otherwise my girlfriend won't spend the night here."

And so for very little money my house transforms, and my spartan life perks up a bit. It builds in flavor like a slow-simmering broth, even though the yellowed paper of the magazines makes my eyes water and there are termites in the portrait. It doesn't bother me, these new acquisitions entertain me, they keep me company. My orphaned neighbor, on the other hand, grows tired of the tedious sale, and maybe also of his only regular client. So one day he shoves it all into a big garbage bin and speeds off to the beach on his motorcycle, with his girlfriend's arms clasped around him for dear life.

At the Cash Register

The idea of spending money, of buying myself something lovely but unnecessary, has always burdened me. Is it because my father would scrupulously count out his coins, and rub his fingers over every bill before giving me one in case there was another stuck to it? Who hated eating out, who wouldn't order even a cup of tea in a coffee bar because a box of tea bags in the supermarket cost the same? Was it my parents' strict tutelage that prompts me to always choose the least-expensive dress, greeting card, dish on the menu? To look at the tag before the item on the rack, the way people look at the descriptions of paintings in a museum before lifting their eyes to the work?

Maybe my father would have liked the bars in my neighborhood, where I can ask for a glass of water filled with bubbles that rise to the top, and sip it slowly while I catch my breath or have a quick chat with someone, without paying a cent.

And yet my father, the only one who earned money in the household, saved up to go to the theater, even springing for decent seats. That money was a type of personal investment for him, something that perhaps kept him sane. My mother, on the other hand, who never worked, and therefore never had any economic independence, always had a twisted relationship to money. I still remember her reproaching me once, years and years ago—I must have been seven or eight—when I wanted a frilly white dress in a store, with short sleeves and a little pearl necklace sewn right around the collar. That detail had enchanted me at the time.

That's too expensive, don't even go near it, she'd told me, irritated. And I felt bad, I felt terrible, not so much because I couldn't have the dress as for having desired something out of reach, for having dared to desire such a thing.

Even more upsetting, a memory from when I was around thirteen. I'd gone out with a younger cousin, and it was my job to keep an eye on her, to be the responsible one. We took a bus into the city—what fun!—to spend the afternoon in a popular, crowded market, and there in the middle of hundreds of booths full of trinkets of every kind I was attracted to a pair of lightweight, dangling earrings: two columns of little plastic pieces, red ones and black ones. Nothing terribly special, but from everything that there was to choose they had caught my eye.

My mother had given me some money and so I'd bought them, satisfied with my purchase, but when I went back home and showed her my new jewelry, my mother, who asked how much I'd spent for them, turned angry, reprimanding me at length, saying, You don't know how to handle money, no one pays that much for a pair of earrings like these, they cheated you. It was one of her typical rants. And after that I was never able to look at those earrings without hating myself.

And now I'm thinking of another important moment, when I was an adult. My first boyfriend was cleaning his room—the room where we would make love and where I lost my virginity—before moving to a new place. He wanted to get rid of the loose coins scattered and forgotten on the ground, under the bed, below the cushion of the armchair. They're not worth much, there's no point in picking them up, he'd said. He'd swept up all those coins along with heaps of dust accumulated for years behind the furniture, and in that moment I understood, with a painful lucidity, that our relationship would have to end.

By now I earn a decent amount and spend money every day without thinking too much about it. But the fear still grips me when I least expect it, if a paperback with an attractive cover catches my eye, or a cheerful plant for the balcony. Objects like this remind me of the red-and-black earrings and paralyze me. That's why, every now and again, even if I'm dying of hunger, I pick the simplest sandwich, or I don't eat, period. If I walk into a store, if I admire something but don't buy it, if I walk out and manage to avoid the cash register, I feel like a virtuous daughter. And if I cave, well, I cave.

Today for instance, a chilly day, I pause in the pharmacy in front of some bottles of body oil. The pharmacist is attentive, patient. She lets me try a few, she introduces me to the various scents: lavender, rose, pomegranate.

"Our skin turns dry in this weather," she says. "You can pour a drop of this right into the bathtub if you like. You need to pamper yourself, *dottoressa*."

But I'm not convinced, I can't justify the expense, surely I've already got something like this in my bathroom. In the end I just ask for the pills I always keep in my purse in case I get a headache.

In My Head

Why does it take me so long to get out of the house this morning? What bewilders me, even here at home? I'm finding it harder and harder to get up and do things right away: react, move, concentrate. Today, as I'm getting ready, without rushing, for an entirely ordinary day, I lose track of myself, I'm hesitant in front of my closet even though I really don't care what I wear. I eat breakfast without sitting down, without enjoying it, I slice up an apple but don't put the slices on a plate, I don't know if I should have another coffee or not, I'm restless, I don't know how to proceed. Fifteen minutes go by, they turn into half an hour.

I'm about to leave but then I stop, I take off my jacket and start looking for a necklace to perk up my dress, it must be here somewhere, in some jewelry box (though I prefer "joy box" for *portagioie*, which, come to think of it, is the most beautiful of Italian words).

I'm flummoxed by this unraveling of time, I'm losing my grip on myself. I know that nothing awful will happen on the other side of the door. If anything, I'm about to have a perfectly forgettable day: a class to teach, a meeting with colleagues, maybe a movie. But I'm afraid of forgetting something crucial—my cell phone or my identity card, my health insurance or my keys. And I'm afraid of running into trouble.

At Dinner

A bachelor friend of mine likes hosting dinners at his house. He lives on the top floor of a building which has a lovely terrace that looks out over cupolas and antennas. It's a charming place to pass the time. But tonight's windy, so we'll eat inside. I take the elevator as far as it goes, then climb a flight of stairs to reach his apartment. He lives in a sort of playhouse, full of tight corners and dark, exposed beams. The rooms, all of them small, lead from one to another, without a hallway. Almost all the rooms have a bed and cushions strewn on the floor, and lots of books, so that at any moment, in any given room, you can sit down and read or take a nap. I think a child would love it here. But my friend, an elegant and learned man in his sixties, never had children.

Because the ceilings are low and sloped we have to duck our heads before taking a seat at my friend's table. "Watch your heads," he always says. The guests tend to vary, apart from a small core of people that includes me. Typically, I don't ever see the others again. He runs a sort of social laboratory that lasts for a few hours and seldom repeats itself.

I came on foot tonight, swallowing mouthfuls of cold air, and I've worked up an appetite. I'm a little late, the others are already sitting on the sofas. I have a glass of wine and eat some peanuts. I say hello to someone who directs films, then a journalist, then a woman who writes poetry, then a psychologist, then a couple from the North who are here to spend their honeymoon.

She irritates me off the bat, maybe because she doesn't bother to look at me when she shakes my hand. She's a woman in her thirties, with a sturdy build, but her face is thin and pointy, as if it belongs to another body. She wears her sleek hair pulled back and her extra pounds look good on her, rendering her appealingly solid.

She talks about the city. She's a bit over the top, she's got an opinion about everything. She interrupts me when I'm in the middle of telling the others what I do for a living. She shifts everyone's attention to a painting over the sofa. She claims she knows the artist personally. He's got some talent, she says, but is overrated. All of her opinions get under my skin, everything she says feels off the mark, even a little impertinent. But at the same time I'm drawn to her energy, she's magnetic, someone who knows how to hold a crowd.

We're eight around the table. After we finish the soup the others stop talking, and she and I carry on. We're discussing a film, which I liked, so I defend it. But she insists that the actor, a famous leading man, gave a terrible performance.

Though I'm not drunk I can't help it, I say:

"Do you realize you have no idea what the fuck you're talking about?"

She doesn't reply, and after that she erases me out of her evening. The others exchange embarrassed glances. I've never exploded like that at a small dinner among friends. The husband looks at me, gelid. I've just attacked the woman he loves and would like to have a family with. Someone changes the subject, but I can't focus anymore. I've stopped eating. My friend clears the table as if nothing happened. He brings out a cake and cups of coffee.

I go home, mortified. I walk back even though I'm exhausted. It takes me forty minutes. I hurry past the dark buildings, the shuttered windows. Even after the long walk I'm jangled, out of sorts. I'll apologize to my friend for spoiling the evening. I cut across the piazza where I'll buy food in the morning. But tonight I ask the teenagers chatting at the base of the fountain if they can spare a cigarette.

On Vacation

I take advantage of a long weekend in the fall and leave the city to clear my head, to enjoy the waning warmth in a nearby town and escape the daily routine. I arrive in a sunlit, peaceful spot. The arrangements are to my liking: the quiet hotel, the tasty breakfast, the pool that's empty until noon. The only problem is that here, too, I feel pressure to do what everyone else does. At breakfast they all talk about the long trails to hike, the pine forest filled with fallow deer, a restaurant at the top of the trail that has spectacular views. There's also the house of a famous writer, a woman, to visit. But I'm not up for any of that, I'd rather sleep, take in the fresh air, swim a few laps before the kids start jumping in.

I never went on vacation with my parents when I was little. I wasn't like the children I see here, with families that eat together and sit around playing cards.

Maybe my father was wise, or maybe he was just

stubborn, but he believed that it was better to relax at home, without packing a suitcase, without the effort of getting used to a new place just for a few days. Half the vacation gets wasted that way, he'd say. So every year, in the weeks he didn't have to go to work, he stayed home. He'd wear his pajamas until late, then he'd go down to the piazza to buy newspapers and say hi to the neighbors who were already retired and sat talking all day on benches. Then he'd lie back on the sofa, in front of a fan, and read the papers, listening to some music. He didn't crave the mountains, or the sea, he wasn't roused by nature's beauty. He was a hermit; true peace, for him, meant staying indoors, staying put in a familiar place.

My mother would have enjoyed traveling, taking trips. She always wanted to go to big cities, to visit museums and sacred places, the temples of the gods. My father found all that exhausting, not to mention a waste of money. He'd say, And what if it rains, that would ruin everything. I don't feel like driving for hours, I'm better off relaxing here at home, or else at the theater. And given that he was the one with a job, and also a driver's license, all three of us stayed home in the summer.

As an adult I've learned to conform to certain customs. I understand why it's important to go away and unplug now and then. I don't mind a change of scene once a year. I never go back to the same place, it's better not to feel tied to one versus the other. But what I end up feeling far from isn't so much the daily grind—it's my family, my childhood. And that distance, as much as I want it, upsets me. I turn melancholy when I lie out in the sun. I mourn my unhappy origins. I feel sad for my mother, frustrated as a wife, disdainful now that she's a widow.

At the same time I see my father's point, there's no denying that this brief vacation puts a strain on my wallet. I wish I had certain possessions with me, to be honest. I'm already tired of having breakfast, dressed, at eight in the morning in the midst of other people. The coffee's tepid, and after the first two days, even though it's off-season, the hotel fills up, with little kids who start jumping in the pool after breakfast, and in the evenings the young couple that run the hotel play music so that the guests can dance under the stars.

After dinner I go to my room and watch television. I think a great deal about my parents, and I ask myself, in this sheltered place, why they're still nipping at my heels.

Which one of them do I take after? My father, who would have stayed in the room to read like me? Or my mother, who would have wanted to dance? She would have enjoyed getting to know people other than my father and myself. The people she adored—friends, relatives, people around whom she laughed heartily, around whom she never sulked—were all people she didn't live with. My father and I were her cage.

At the Supermarket

There's no food in my refrigerator, so I head to the supermarket, where I bump into my married friend for whom I represent . . . what, exactly? A road not taken, a hypothetical affair? I carry a basket with a few things inside, the routine purchases of a woman on her own, while he pushes a cart overflowing with all kinds of food: cereal boxes, bags of biscuits and cookies and melba toast, jams, butter, whole milk, skim milk, soy milk. He tells me what each member of the family likes to eat, the ongoing battle to sit down to breakfast together, something which, to his regret, rarely happens. He likes to have ample stores in the pantry: boxes of rice and pasta, cans of chickpeas and tomatoes, containers of coffee and sugar, bottles of oil, bottles of still and sparkling water.

"In case disaster strikes," he says, kidding.

"Why would there be a disaster?"

With or without the food, I doubt a disaster will ever take place in that home. I never stock up, I shop from day to day. My refrigerator is never full, neither is my pantry.

We pay up at the register, separately. It takes him fifteen minutes to put all that food into shopping bags. I follow him down to the parking lot below the supermarket. We escape the banal music, the neon lights, the odor of food, the excessive air-conditioning.

"Can I give you a ride?"

"I don't have much to carry, I can walk."

"It's supposed to rain, let's head back together."

He opens the trunk. All the shopping bags, made of a sickly transparent green, look alike and merge into one big mass. We decide to put my two bags in one of the car seats. It's a little disgusting, covered with crumbs, and around it I see the detritus left by his children, imprisoned for long journeys in that car: all manner of toys, dismembered action figures, battered books.

He pulls a chocolate bar out of one of his bags.

"We need to eat this right away," he says.

I know the reason. My friend, his wife, is worried about his blood sugar, his intake of saturated fats. He gives me a little piece.

"No one knows about this parking lot. See how

empty it is? I like to keep it a secret, I never tell anyone that I know about it."

He drops me off at my door. I take my bags, thank
him, and say goodbye, kissing him on the cheeks like
always.

"Sure you don't need anything else? Want a few of
our bags? Half of it's just stuff for the pantry."

"If disaster strikes, I'd suggest you abandon the
house."

"You're probably right about that."

In any case, I don't need anything else. The tender-
ness he sets aside for me is enough.

By the Sea

I'm in a restaurant in the little town along the
coast. Through the glass I can see the sky—it's
gray today—and the sea. It's a wintry Sunday, still
a nice day, with not too much wind. The sun's hidden
but at least there's no rain.

We've gathered for the baptism of the daughter of
one of my colleagues with whom I'm friendly. She
told me it meant a lot to her, so I said yes, even though
to be honest I was tempted to decline the invitation.
Another colleague of ours gave me a ride. He's irritat-
ing, but unfortunately, I don't have a car.

After the ceremony in the church we came to the
restaurant. We're a big group, and three long tables
occupy most of the space. The whole restaurant has
been reserved just for us. It's clear that the owners
know my friend's family well—they've celebrated
other important occasions here and feel at home.
Most of the guests are relatives of either my friend

or her husband: the parents, cousins, in-laws, aunts and uncles, other children. The little girl sleeps in her pram in spite of the racket. The laughter swells and dies down like the waves that crash on the beach in front of us.

I see the cousins of this newly baptized baby, those who are older, those who can walk, those able to eat on their own, those who are eating so much they could probably already stand to lose a kilo or two.

We raise our glasses and make a toast, and then the lunch is served. The waiters bring a vast array of appetizers to the tables—mussels, clams, anchovies, cheese, olives, smoked tuna, shrimp—all on individual plates. I've chosen a seat far from the tedious colleague who gave me a ride, with whom I'll have to ride back soon enough.

I eat and drink a little wine. I talk with the people seated on either side of me. I explain who I am and how I know my friend and what I do for work. I look at the moody sky above the sea, the blurry horizon where sea and sky meet, the great peace that lies beyond this confusion. I'm struck that I'm the only one in the room admiring the sea's splendor at this moment.

Though we're crowded together I feel separate from the group, excluded from their enduring, unquestioned bonds. On the other hand, I feel obligated to pay attention to people I barely know. I feel a bit off physically as well. I'm making an effort just to sit here, and I'm oddly aware of the weight of my head on my neck. There's nothing in my throat but I'm convinced something is blocking it all the same. I take a breath and observe that my stomach rises and falls, but my chest feels clamped, I need to get out, get some fresh air.

I look around, searching for something to focus on, a steady point. The little girl has woken up, I see her in the arms of my friend's husband. She's crying. Her grandmother comes to comfort her.

I get up. I look for the restroom. I'm told it's outside, and this makes me happy, it means I'm forced to get out of this space.

"It's turned cold, signora. I'd advise a jacket," the waiter says.

I take my coat, go to the bathroom, then sneak off, heading down to the beach. The restless sea is magnificent. I come upon the remains of the home of an emperor. I can vaguely make out the dimensions, the outlines of the rooms that once looked out at the sea, when the emperor lived here in summer.

I think about the little girl and this afternoon in her honor. She's ignorant of the cheerful party organized to celebrate her life, she knows nothing yet about the world.

From down below, the restaurant, brightened by artificial light, seems like an aquarium full of people. They're all dressed in different colors, all moving slowly.

By now I'm not the only one on the beach. A number of the kids have also fled from that glass cube. They run along the shore, shouting out and throwing stones. They hide in the grottoes, among the enduring traces of an uninhabited villa.

Outside, there's a ferocious noise coming from the crashing of the waves and the roar of the wind: a perpetual agitation, a thundering boom that devours everything. I wonder why we find it so reassuring.

At the Coffee Bar

Never married, but like all women, I've had my share of married men. Today I think of one I met here, in this bar on the other side of the river where I now happen to be, on my own. That day I'd had a coffee and I was about to head out. He'd followed me, he'd stopped me on the sidewalk. He'd run like a lunatic behind me.

It was the first time a man had pursued me so vehemently. I'm attractive enough, but not the kind of beauty to make heads turn. And yet he'd said, panting for breath, "Sorry to bother you, but I'd like to get to know you."

That was the gist of it. He was about fifty years old and I was in my twenties. He'd looked at me, fixing me with pale, anxious eyes, not saying anything else. His gaze was kind, also insistent. My impulse was to brush him off and yet I was flattered, he didn't strike me as the type who does nothing but chase after women.

"Just a coffee," he'd added.

"I just had one, I've got some things to do."

"Later on then, around five? I'll wait for you here."

That afternoon I met up with a girlfriend. I told her what had happened.

"What was he like? Were you into him?"

"I'm not sure. Maybe."

"Good-looking? Well-dressed?"

"I'd say so."

"Well then?"

At five-twenty I went back to the bar. He was seated at a small table, waiting, as if he were expecting someone at the airport, waiting and doing nothing else. I'll never forget the warmth in his eyes when he saw me walk in. He was unhappily, permanently married. We had a fling. He lived in another city, and he would come down from time to time, for the day, for work. What else is there to say?

A few faltering memories. Some trips outside the city at lunchtime, in his car. He liked to drive, take a random exit and find a tiny place in the country-side to have a good meal. A series of empty trattorie come to mind. One time it was just the two of us, the waiter, the padrone, the cook who remained behind the scenes. We'd lingered all afternoon, talking. I don't remember what we ate, just the abundance and variety of the food that surrounded us, as if it were a lavish wedding.

They'd let him smoke at the table. I had no idea where he lived with his wife, I never asked which city he returned to. He never came to my place. I waited for his phone call and showed up for every date. It was an incendiary time, a momentary surge that has nothing to do with me anymore.

At the Villa

There's a villa near my house that once belonged to a wealthy family, with grounds that attract children and dogs. I like to go in the late morning to walk along the shaded paths. I pass a giant birdcage, as large as a two-story house, with a lovely cupola at the top. It no longer contains birds. Pigeons, filthy and fierce, arrange themselves on the cupola like barbs on a wire. Parrots with their bright-green feathers flit from tree to tree, landing briefly on the grass. The fountain inside the birdcage is covered with moss that's the same green as the parrot feathers. The water from the fountain never ceases to flow.

The path is lined with other fountains, as well as statues of unsettling creatures that don't exist: female forms with four breasts, a woman who turns into a lion from the stomach down. Satyrs, hairy below the waist, with goat hooves, carry urns on their shoulders. The women all pose like beasts, languid and provocative. Ecstatic children with fishtails blow into conches.

The villa itself is always closed, but through beautiful windows I see dark wooden tables, chairs, shelves full of books. It looks like a library, or an institute of some kind, but there's no sign outside, it's got a secretive air. I bet it's nice to sit inside and read a book. But I've never seen a soul.

Today as I'm walking I come across two people, a man and a woman. I'm guessing they're in their seventies. They step down together, gingerly, in a spot where the path is rather uneven, the ground furrowed as if by a stream. They're clearly well-acquainted, but they don't strike me as husband and wife. Something tells me they are brother and sister, with a childhood in common, an intimacy that was imposed and indisputable.

As I approach them I realize that every step the woman takes is an effort. Then I notice a draining mechanism that emerges from her belly. Two tubes, two plastic sacks. One is full of blood and the other holds a liquid, relatively clear but viscous. She's wearing sunglasses with oversized, rectangular black lenses; I can't make out her expression. Nevertheless, she seems incredibly powerful. She was probably operated on a few days ago. There's a hospital behind the villa, maybe she's still a patient there, or maybe she's just been discharged, and is feeling reassured but also dazed by the outside world.

The man, let's call him her brother, walks beside her and supports her. Their bodies are almost attached. He holds the tubes, long and thin, in his hand; they're like leashes for the dogs that run free at this time of day.

The elderly woman looks more alive to me than the children shouting and playing on the grass. I'm moved by the sight of these two people, literally tied to one another. It's astonishing. It speaks of the devotion, the vital connection between them. I think about the substances that flow inside our bodies, which need to circulate, which need to be eliminated at intervals. All those hidden functions, ugly and essential.

They don't speak, they just walk, carefully. I think of her regaining consciousness in the recovery room after the anesthesia wore off, after a grueling procedure. She'd slept through it, stretched out on the table, feeling none of it, someplace else.

In the Country

I decide to spend a few days in the country house of my friend, the one who's always traveling. She noticed that I was feeling down one day and said, "It's free, there's nothing to stress you out there, it will do you good." And given that I'm going through a hard patch right now, I accepted her invitation. I pack a bag and catch a train from the central station. I stare up at all the destinations one might go, listed on the big board, and I think of all the places I might still visit, and how arbitrary one's own path is. It's a short trip. I get off before reaching the end of the newspaper. A car's been left for me in the parking lot, by the gardener.

This landscape, these hills dotted with castles, must be a dream in summer. It's been a while since I've driven, but I'm comfortable behind the wheel. It's a small, sturdy car. The road keeps taking me uphill. I follow my friend's advice and stop in town to buy food for three days so that I don't need to go out again. When I tell the shopkeepers that I'm staying at my friend's place they grow friendly, letting me taste the cheeses before I buy. They all say it's about to turn brutally cold: three days in a row of low temperatures, fierce winds, maybe even a little snow.

The house is in the valley and the views are breathtaking, the sky wide and bright. I can only see a handful of other houses in the distance. A tarp covers the pool, the hammock trembles between two trees, and the desiccated vines of the pergola need a good trimming.

I retrieve the spare key kept under a rock and open the door. I unpack my bag, build a fire, then prepare coffee. It's a big country kitchen with a marble sink bathed with light that pours in through the window. Terra-cotta cookware, jugs and jars painted by hand. High up, just below the ceiling, there's a row of iron keys mounted to the wall, forming a long, illegible epigraph. Superfluous keys that opened doors that no longer exist.

I put on my sneakers and go out for a walk before sunset. I follow the path that cuts through the wheat fields. There's no mayhem here, it's a tranquil corner of the world, with everything in its place, the hay neatly gathered in big circular bales. An area that's resisted change, that remains unspoiled. I walk as far as a creek, check my watch, and then turn back. Solitude demands a precise assessment of time, I've always understood this. It's like the money in your wallet: you have to know how much time you need to kill, how much to spend before dinner, what's left over before going to bed. But time seems different here. My walk took an hour, but to me it felt much longer.

In the evening I cook for myself. When I'm in the city I usually buy prepared food in a store near my house, a simple can of good tuna and a fork might do, but I'm inspired to make a real meal here, even one that requires a bit of effort. I arrange a few chicken thighs in a baking pan, adorning them with springs of thyme, garlic cloves, salt, slices of lemon. I slide the pan into the oven. I like the crockery in this house, the thick yellow plates and the thin transparent glasses. I like the books, I leaf through catalogues of art exhibits in the city. I ignore the books I brought to keep me company. I always prefer being surrounded by things that don't belong to me.

After dinner I read in front of the fireplace, nodding off now and then. I listen to their music and leaf through magazines from a year ago. I choose the daughter's room to sleep in, where there's a single bed, and the roof slants low over my head. In the closet, where the comforter is stored, I notice a few hoodies, a basket of bathing suits. I prefer this cozy space to the master bedroom, with its canopy bed of dark heavy wood.

The second day it's even colder, and as I walk through the wheat field the ground is so hard that it no longer yields beneath my feet. The wind blows as I walk, and the lights in the distant houses make me sad. On the way back I feel the weight of being alone here, of not knowing a soul.

Before entering the house I notice something on the path. A small gray creature. I know it's dead, and I, too, immediately stiffen. It's a mouse. Even though I turn my head away I've already seen enough: the delicate, curved tail and the dense, soft coat of fur. But the really disturbing thing is that it's missing a head. It's been sliced off. How? And why? Was it another animal that did it? Some savage bird? The decapitated body revolts me, but at the same time it makes me think of a fig, and as I stand there in the freezing cold I think of the fruit I love most in high summer, and the spectacular red of its sweet sun-warmed flesh.

The animal is motionless, but something is churning inside me. The creature can't harm me, but I'm terrified. In an instant, it stamps out the calm and quiet of this place.

I ask myself why the cut is so precise, as if the head really had been cut off with a knife. Is there another animal prowling around, with jaws capable of this? And why just the head, instead of eating the whole thing? But more important, I ask myself why I'm reacting so intensely to what lies before me. It's a tiny dead animal, that's all. Last night I'd rubbed olive oil over chicken thighs without getting the least bit upset. That raw, lifeless meat hadn't disturbed me. The blood that stained the baking pan here and there was a perfectly normal thing.

I don't want to look at this creature, or touch it. I only want to be as far from it as possible and erase its image from my mind. I wonder if I should just get into the car and head back to the city. But I have to deal with it, there's no one who might help, I can't justify calling the gardener to lend me a hand, that would be pathetic. I walk quickly past the creature, looking the other way. I'm flattened with the absurd terror that he might spring back to life and—now we're talking about a fear that's even more absurd—grab hold of me, cling to me, kill me.

Inside, I look for something to cover him. I find a

can of peeled tomatoes, which I empty out and rinse
well. Now I need something thin and flat to slide
underneath and scoop it up. I find a cardboard box
and cut out a square piece with a pair of scissors.
That's how I'll go about it. But I avoid it, first I make
myself a cup of tea. My little task fills me with dread,
it saps me of energy.

Eventually I step out holding the can and the piece
of cardboard. I remove the lid of the garbage pail and
open the bag tied up inside. I cover the animal with
the can, looking away the whole time, rattled. He's
devoid of life but I'm sweating, my heart's beating fast
and my hands are shaking. Once he's covered, he has
a little less power over me. I kneel down and slowly
slide the piece of cardboard under the can, but right
away there's resistance, I need to nudge it slightly,
insisting bit by bit so that the creature slides onto
its little cardboard carpet. I do all this without ever
glancing at the can.

I stand up holding my contraption, deeply aware,
for a few seconds, of the animal's weight. A few ounces
that tip the balance, they plunge me to the depths. I
realize he's shifting in there. I carry the improvised
casket over to the garbage pail and I throw it into the
open bag, which I subsequently close. The cadaver
vanishes, but when I return to the path I see that a few

drops of blood have spilled from its body during the maneuver.

At night, thank goodness, it rains, and the next day, thanks to the sun, the bloodstain also vanishes. But that poor decapitated mouse, freshly killed, still reminds me of a fig in high summer: the flavor of its red flesh, the warmth in my mouth.

In Bed

This evening as I read in bed I hear the roar of cars that speed down the road below my apartment. And the fact of their passing makes me aware of my own stillness. I can only fall asleep when I hear them. And when I wake up in the middle of the night, always at the same time, it's the absolute silence that interrupts my sleep. That's the hour when there's not a single car on the road, when no one needs to get anywhere. My sleep grows lighter and lighter and then it abandons me entirely. I wait until someone, anyone, drives by. The thoughts that come to roost in my head in those moments are always the gloomiest, also the most precise. That silence, combined with the black sky, takes hold over me until the first light returns and dispels those thoughts, until I hear the presence of lives passing by along the road below me.

On the Phone

Today one of my lovers keeps calling. He presses a key by mistake and reaches me without realizing it. I see his number on my cell phone, I say hello, and he's already talking, enthusiastically, only not to me. I hear him while he's having lunch, while he's asking the waiter what the specials are, while he's walking down the street, while he's at the office. His roaming voice ends up in my ear, distant but familiar, present, absent. He's laughing as he's talking. While I'm privy to all this, he has no clue.

I'm at home today, I don't have plans. I'm constantly cold, it's that patch of autumn before my building turns the heat on, so I've put on a heavy sweater and I keep boiling water for tea. Even in bed, in spite of the down comforter, the sheets radiate no warmth whatsoever. They feel like a punishing slab under my bare feet.

Every time the phone rings I pick up, thinking maybe this time he really is trying to call me. But he's not calling me, he doesn't hear me saying hello, he's still not aware of our ongoing, inadvertent contact.

Who is he talking to? Where is he? I have no idea. He's at work, at a bar, on the platform of the metro, I suppose. It's just that every time I get one of his calls I feel betrayed. Our communication, of which he's ignorant, nettles me. It makes me feel particularly alone.

Finally, in the late afternoon, he calls: it's really him. I pick up and hear the passion in his voice.

"Hi, darling, how are you?"

"Ciao, how was your day?"

"A drag. I was at work all day, I even skipped lunch, it was one thing after another. How about you?"

"My day was also a bit of a drag."

"So what about dinner tonight?"

"Tonight I think I'll pass."

"Why?"

"I've had a headache for hours," I tell him, then hang up and step out, ravenous, to eat dinner on my own. There's no bite to the air; it was colder inside than out.

In the Shade

Yesterday we turned our clocks back an hour, and today it's already dark as I cross the bridge that takes me home. So I'm thinking back to a bright afternoon on a tiny square of burning sand. All the beach umbrellas were taken, it had felt like the whole town was in the water.

I'd gone there for a wedding. The following day, instead of returning home I stayed on, I wanted a day at the beach. I craved a swim even though I didn't have a towel, or sunscreen, even though, to be honest, the beach wasn't that nice. It was narrow, like certain rooms, flanked by two rows of big black rocks full of sharp edges. The water was choppy and the white foam felt blinding. There was a mother standing in front of me. She was short, sturdy, with dark hair. Her children surrounded her, she had at least four. I still remember that she carried a naked baby in her arms. The daughter was pretty, like her mother, but life had

yet to wear her out. I didn't see the father, but the
mother was a steady pillar in the midst of that roil-
ing force. They were all at ease in the furious sea, they
frolicked in it, even the little ones were fearless. They
leaped through the waves at just the right moments,
the same waves that kept knocking me down. I never
managed to get past the point they broke in order to
actually enter the water and swim.

I returned to the shore, which was full of exposed,
sluggish bodies, where I managed to find a spot between one lounge chair and another. The sun was so
strong I thought I might die. My only objective was to
block its rays, or to move into the shade, any patch
of shade, as if it were one of those huge rocks to grab
onto in the middle of the sea. Bit by bit I edged toward
another woman, who slept, unaware of my suffering. Her body exuded an enviable harmony with her
surroundings. Her head was turned to one side, her
eyes were closed, and the red strip of her bikini top
was untied. I lacked her serenity, but her presence
afforded me some relief, and feeling slightly guilty, I
dozed off in her shadow.

When I woke up the lounge chair was empty, the
woman was gone. But the gray light that pervaded the
sky after sunset made me melancholy. That diffuse
shade, exclusive to no one, defeated me, it provided

no relief. Come to think of it, there's always some savage element at the beach, either to tolerate or to overcome: an element we crave and cower from at the same time.

I've always felt in someone's shadow, even though I don't have to compare myself to brothers who are smarter, or to sisters who are prettier.

There's no escape from the shadows that mount, inexorably, in this darkening season. Nor can we escape the shadows our families cast. That said, there are times I miss the pleasant shade a companion might provide.

In Winter

At the end of the year, when all the schoolchildren in the city are on vacation, I accept
an invitation to accompany my friends and
their children—the son and daughter—on a visit to a
castle. He drives. He's my friend from the bridge,
the one quarreling on the street, the one from the
supermarket. His wife should have been with us,
but she's come down with a bad cold and has decided,
at the last minute, to stay home. So I stand in for her
today.

On our way back to the city we stop to stretch our
legs in a sleepy little town. He parks in front of a
precipice. We get out of the car and walk up the narrow road, seeking glimpses of sunlight. A woman
sweeps the piazza—two crisscrossed flags and a small
fountain—with a broom. She goes about it as if that
public space were her own living room.

We continue walking. The children run on ahead.

We linger under a grand house that looms over the countryside. At the base of a statue, we read the name of the noble family that once owned it. It's a stone facade, but the colors are a mix of pale pink, yellow, and orange—warm shades that form the background for the slanting shadows cast by lampposts. The town, practically abandoned this afternoon, starts to drown in a piercing light.

We're doubled over by a sharp wind and our eyes are filled with tears. We see the church at the top of the hill, and an ancient olive tree decorated with shiny red balls, in place of a Christmas tree. The higher we climb, the more we feel the wind and the cold. We're enfolded by the wide-open space, enclosed by all that emptiness.

We pause at one of the side streets, curious to see where it leads. It's actually a dead end, a sort of courtyard composed of four buildings, or maybe it's just one building with three or four separate entrances. It's a sheltered space, so dark that it's an effort to adjust our eyes. But bit by bit we make out a staircase with a railing that leads to a brick archway, and a few doors, closed and battered. The winter sunset seeps in through some cracks. It's incredible, it feels as if we're standing in a grotto, with light that darts through it like fish.

As soon as I step into that secluded niche I dream of inhabiting it, of withdrawing there, away from everything. He's standing beside me, we admire it together, and before heading out he turns to look at me. "Stunning," he says. The word burns inside me but I can't tell if he's talking about me or the place we're in. He's enigmatic that way, and in any case, in spite of today's jaunt, in theory romantic, I don't feel many sparks between us.

His daughter wants a hot chocolate, so we walk back to the town, hoping to find a bar that's open. The woman with the broom says, "Ask down that way," and we proceed to a barbershop, which, to our surprise, has numerous clients inside. "At the top of that road, in about three hundred meters," a man tells us, reclining in his chair, his face covered with soap.

We walk to the top of the road but alas, the bar is closed. The large awning, which still needs to be taken down for the season, whips wildly in the wind.

We go back to the car parked in front of the precipice. And as he turns on the engine and shifts into reverse I feel a panic starting to rise, not trusting that low cement barrier between us and the abyss. I don't trust that the car will move backward, all I feel is the steep downward slope, pointing toward danger. But we go up, the car whines as it pulls out in reverse gear and we move, against the force of gravity, away from the little town with its spotlessly clean piazza, and the hushed grotto that enchanted me, and the man who will have dinner tonight, freshly shaved. No hot chocolate, just the depleting artificial heat inside the car. We go home without talking, though the little girl hums strange songs to herself all the while.

At the Stationer's

My beloved stationery store is in the heart of the city, in a beautiful old building built on the corner of two busy streets. I make a trip at the end of every year to buy my agenda, which happens to be my favorite purchase, and which has turned into a sort of rite, but apart from that I like to stop by nearly every week to pick up, who knows, a transparent folder, or sticky page markers, or a new eraser that has yet to wipe anything out. I poke through the colored notebooks and try out the inks of various pens on a piece of paper trampled by countless unknown signatures and urgent, agitated scribbles. I ask for spare paper for my printer at home and boxes to organize my life's paper trail: letters, bills, jottings. Even when I don't need anything in particular I stop in front of the window to admire the display, which always appears so festive, decked with backpacks, scissors, tacks, glue, Scotch tape, and piles of little notebooks, with and without lines on their pages. I'd like to fill them all up, even that unwelcoming accounts ledger. Even though I can't draw, I'd like one of those sketchbooks, hand bound, with thick cream-colored paper.

Through the window I can also observe the family that owns the store. The mother, a rotund woman with dark, dry hair, sits at the register. The father oversees the fountain pens stored in a glass case, as if they were precious jewels, bottles of ink lined up like costly perfumes. The parents are always talking to their lanky son, dressed in black, who clambers up the ladder in two seconds to bring down this or that from the shelves. A lively, intelligent debate is their way of communicating. They comment on articles in the newspaper that the mother is always leafing through, the crazy things that happen every day in the city, the great difficulties facing countries they'll never visit.

I'm especially fond of the mother. One time I thought I'd left my sunglasses in the store. I rushed back, and when I told her what I was missing she stepped down from the cash register right away, accompanying me carefully through the store, stopping in front of the shelves, retracing my steps. I'd bought a lot that day but she'd kept track of it all, she still had each purchase in her head, which is why she led the way without asking me a thing.

"I don't see them here, honey," she'd said at the end of her investigation, but then, giving me a hard look, she conveyed that the sunglasses were attached to the collar of my coat, hanging like a bat behind my scarf.

This stationery store has been one of my haunts for years. When I was a young girl I'd go there to get what I needed for school, then for college, and now for teaching. Every purchase, however mundane, makes me happy. Each item validates my life somehow.

But today when I get here all I see are suitcases in the window, all hard-shelled, most of them the right size to carry on board for a quick getaway by plane. They're all on deep discount. Inside, they've taken down the high shelves, and in the middle of that space there are more suitcases, some bigger, arranged by color and manufacturer. There's nothing harmonious about this, the store looks hideous. In spite of the high ceiling and the graceful proportions it's turned ugly, bereft of character. It reminds me of that disorderly part of the airport where orphaned suitcases gather once they come off the conveyor belt, knowing that no one will come to claim them.

I grow sad looking at all those brand-new suitcases, all of them empty, waiting for a traveler, waiting for various things to fill them, waiting for someplace to go. There's nothing else for sale. Just suitcases. But then, right at the entrance, I notice a bunch of umbrellas, big ones and small ones, of the cheapest quality, bait for desperate tourists caught in a downpour, those pathetic umbrellas that almost always end up in the garbage can after the storm, shoved in with a certain fury, looking like tortured herons.

The family that ran the stationery store isn't in charge of this place, I don't see them. There's just a languid young man with fine features who looks halfheartedly through the store window, out onto the street and at the passing cars. I feel like walking in and asking, Where's the family? I wonder if the business failed, if they were evicted, humiliated, if they'd been upset. But it's not this young man's fault. He's just here to make a living. As disappointed as I am, I'm not surprised that my beloved stationery store no longer exists, the rents must be sky-high around here, and furthermore, who buys notebooks in the end? My students can barely write by hand, they press buttons to learn about life and explore the world. Their thoughts emerge on screens and dwell inside clouds that have no substance, no shortage of space.

A couple comes in: they're young and in love, attached at the hip, that sublime phase when every stupid thing feels enchanting. The store doesn't upset these two, on the contrary, it's clear that this is just the place they've been looking for. They get pleasurably lost in that warren of luggage. They open and close the brand-new models, lined, unlined, pulling on the zippers, pounding plastic carapaces. It's probably the first time they're going away together. Maybe also the last? Will they come to the conclusion, after spending three days together in a hotel, that they're not really so in love? Or will their bond only deepen? As I contemplate this, the suitcases turn, for a few seconds, into enormous books: they're swollen volumes lacking titles, lacking meaning, collected in a library for monsters, or for idiots.

She picks out a purple suitcase. He decides on bright yellow. They pay the young man, then put their new luggage to the test, placing a few shopping bags inside, along with the jackets and scarves they don't need given that, after a coolish morning, the day has turned suddenly warm and everyone on the street is peeling off layers. These two appear quite satisfied, eager for their voyage together. They leave the store dragging behind them, on four spinning wheels, an unquestionable joy that furrows the worn-down cobblestones of the city.

At Dawn

If I go up to the roof of my building I can see the sun rise. Usually I'm too lazy, I hate leaving the warmth of my bed, so it's hard to get it together, get up, get dressed in time. But in winter, every so often, I manage, given that the day starts a little later. I throw my coat over my pajamas, and tie a scarf, and pull on a pair of boots, then I take the elevator and have a seat among all the laundry that the other tenants in the building hang out to dry, between towels and tablecloths, sweaters and underwear. I wait as the golden light highlights a section of the jagged contours of the hills across the way. It all happens in a matter of seconds: the sphere, so precise at the start, emerges, perfectly round, like an egg yolk that then slips from its shell. It rises methodically, turning pale as it climbs higher, though I know it's not budging, not even by a millimeter, that it's just an illusion, fantastical. I watch until it's no longer possible, until it becomes too painful.

But it's not just my eyes that suffer at dawn, it's my heart that breaks. I feel the light that blazes across the city, striking my face but also warming my marrow, and as it rises I continue to look at my neighbors' laundry, threadbare and bone-dry. Then I close my eyes so that I see the light through my eyelids, and I regret being typically sluggish and missing out on this extraordinary, everyday phenomenon. On the other hand, I couldn't bear beginning each morning like this. I'm both ablaze with energy and sapped of it, and I remember the words of a great writer underlined in one of my books: *I flee, after a moment, terrified, from the great flame to the shadows: I fear the flame will consume me, that it will seize me and reduce me to an element even less significant on this earth, a worm or a plant . . . I can't think straight, everything seems futile, life itself seems extremely simple, I don't care if nobody thinks of me anymore, if hardly anyone writes to me.* Feeling similarly depleted, I return downstairs and write these lines as another day begins.

In My Head

I t's that spring in my step I've always lacked, an absence of agility that would hold me back, that was an obstacle when I was a young girl, at school. For half an hour they let us play outside. Most of the students were euphoric during that short block of time, but I couldn't stand it. I hated their sharp cries, the spontaneous exaltation. In any case, the game I'd play with my friends back then was to leap from one tree stump to another, as if they were little round islands, a wooden archipelago arranged in a clearing. The stumps were low, they must have come up to our hips, no higher than that, but climbing on top of them made me sick to my stomach, and once I stood up my legs would tremble. Crossing those gaps cautiously and clumsily to get from one to the other took enormous effort, one that humiliated me as the other girls moved back and forth without a thought, relishing every second of the activity as if they were birds hopping from branch to branch. How I envied their brazen strides. It now occurs to me that I was as tenacious as I was timid. I never protested, I did what they did, that is, I clambered up, I hesitated, and then I strode across, afraid each time that the empty space between the stumps would swallow me up, terrified each time that I would fall, even though I never did.

At His Place

Ever since that trip together with his children I've been feeling off-kilter. I've wondered what it would be like to take things further, and I think, too often, about the way he laughs, the way his voice reverts to the high pitch of a little boy's, and the hairs on his wrists and scattered on the backs of his hands, and the humorous messages he still sends me now and then. I wait but he doesn't get in touch, it's been a while since I've seen him in the neighborhood, but then one day the phone rings, and his name on the screen already smacks of impudence. My friend is usually at work at this hour, their children are at school. What will he suggest this time? A bite to eat at the bar on the corner?

Instead when I hear his voice I realize something's happened. He explains it all quickly: my friend's father has had a stroke and the outlook is grim. They got the call early in the morning and they left the dog and the house without tending to either. The barista on the corner has the keys.

I head over right away, the dog needs to go out. It's the first time I've been at their place alone. Until now all I've known is the table set for a dinner, the bathroom used by guests, the kitchen crowded with pots and pans. This morning it's all under control in spite of the call before dawn, the hasty departure. The plates in the dishwasher are clean, and the coffee-pot on the stove is the only thing to wash. Someone spilled a bit of sugar on the countertop.

I look into the bedrooms. The bright one, unclut-tered, with white linen curtains, that he shares with my friend, and the one right next to it, less spacious, crowded with toys and a bunk bed. But even there, it's all relatively tidy. The hallway is lined with photos of the two of them and of the children, photos of the four of them, moments of parenting they treasure, with their children at the seaside, or abroad, or in their laps. I pull down a few window shades and turn off the lever for the gas. I spread a blanket over the bed. I tie the garbage bag. This is the private morphology of a family, of two people who fall in love and have chil-dren: an enterprise as mundane as it is utterly spe-cific. And all at once I see how they form an ingenious organism, an impenetrable collective.

I find the leash that hangs by the door and take the dog out. I walk him to the villa behind my house, carrying a few plastic bags in my pocket. We walk past the dirty fountains, beneath the sclerotic palms, past the pockmarked statues flecked with lichen and moss.

He's a good dog, it doesn't take long for him to trust me. He doesn't bark, he leads me along the grounds of the villa, and I like the tinkling of the tags around his collar. He stops to drink water from a fountain, in front of a she-lion who crushes a skull with her paw, and another, recumbent, eating an apple.

Three times a day, for the next three days, until they've buried my friend's father, until they come back, the dog and I make the same rounds. I grow fond of the animal, of his ears, always alert, and of his careful gait, his determined muzzle. Our walks together thrust me forward, and though he pulls me, I'm the one holding the leash. Every step puts distance between me and my infatuation until it's no longer dangerous, until our romance, which never took hold to begin with, loses its hold over me.

At the Coffee Bar

"What's new?" my barista asks one day.

"I'm thinking of leaving for a while."

"What do you mean?"

"I've received a fellowship to go to a place I've never been before."

"What would you do there?"

"I'd work on my own in the mornings. Then twice a day I'd sit at a long table to eat lunch and dinner with other scholars. I'd get to know them, have discussions, that sort of thing."

"Sounds nice. And how long would this last?"

"A year."

"You're torn about it?"

"I've never left this city."

"This city is a big fat drag."

I finish my coffee and leaf distractedly through the newspaper someone else has left behind, and at one point, toward the bottom of the page, I recognize a face: the curly mass of hair, the large limpid eyes, the fine features. It's the philosopher who was next door to me in that dreadful hotel. He's probably accepted lots of invitations like the one I'm considering. Maybe it's a sign.

I'm pleased to come across him again, to recall our riding up and down the elevator together, our unspoken accord. I still mean to read one of his books.

I remember how he used to speak excitedly in a foreign language, one I never managed to identify. In the picture he's got that same smile, polite but ironic, ever so slightly malicious, that had somehow withstood the tedium of the conference. I haven't forgotten his generous gaze, at once absent and piercing.

Below the picture there's a block of text, just one column. I assume it's an article about him, maybe a review of his latest book. After a long illness, it says. I'd had no idea.

Upon Waking

Today when I wake up I stay put. I don't go to the bathroom to weigh myself or to the kitchen to drink a glass of tepid water before preparing the coffeepot. The city doesn't beckon or lend me a shoulder today. Maybe it knows I'm about to leave. The sun's dull disk defeats me; the dense sky is the same one that will carry me away. That vast and vaporous territory, lacking precise pathways, is all that binds us together now. But it never preserves our tracks. The sky, unlike the sea, never holds on to the people that pass through it. The sky contains nothing of our spirit, it doesn't care. Always shifting, altering its aspect from one moment to the next, it can't be defined.

This morning I'm scared. I'm afraid to leave this house, this neighborhood, this urban cocoon. But I've already got one foot out the door. The suitcases, purchased at my former stationery store, are already packed. I just need to lock them now. I've given the key to my subletter and I've told her how often she needs to water the plants, and how the handle of the door to the balcony sometimes sticks. I've emptied out one closet and locked another, inside of which I've amassed everything I consider important. It's not much in the end: notebooks, letters, some photos and papers, my diligent agendas. As for the rest, I don't really care, though it does occur to me that for the first time someone else will be using my cups, dishes, forks, and napkins on a daily basis.

Last night at dinner, at a friend's house, everyone wished me well, telling me to have a wonderful time. They hugged me and said, Good luck!

He wasn't there, he had other plans. I had a nice time anyway, we lingered at the table, still talking after midnight.

I tell myself: A new sky awaits me, even though it's the same as this one. In some ways it will be quite grand. For an entire year, for example, I won't have to shop for food, or cook, or do the dishes. I'll never have to eat dinner by myself.

I might have said no, I might have just stayed put. But something's telling me to push past the barrier

At My Mother's

Twice a month I take the train to see her, after lunch. Each time I bring a small box of cat's tongue cookies from the bakery around the corner, even though they always threaten to break apart. Today, the first day of a new year, I bring her another dozen, wrapped up on a gilt-colored cardboard tray.

The day is cloudy. Last night, after the fireworks, it rained. Now I see sheep through the train window, they're stock-still against the rolling hills. At the station I take a bus that climbs the road leading to her town. By now I'm on friendly terms with the driver. He's a bit cheeky, some might even call him a pain in the ass, but he doesn't get on my nerves. To be honest I sort of welcome our typical, extravagant exchange.

"Signora, you're looking spectacular," he tells me today. "That's one lucky husband you've got. Not that of my life, just like the dog that pulled me along the paths of the villa. And so I heed my call, having come to know the guts and soul of this place a little too well. It's just that today, feeling slothful, I'm prey to those embedded fears that don't dissipate.

he'd ever admit it, or am I mistaken? May you prosper heartily in the new year."

The bus hugs the walls, rattling as it goes. I'm the only passenger. I get off at the piazza where my mother has decided to grow old, on the third floor of a building on top of a pharmacy. Her caretaker opens the door and leaves almost as soon as I step inside.

My mother is sitting in her armchair in front of the television. She's gotten dressed, she looks even thinner, even smaller. The maroon cardigan I gave her last year hangs on her, barely grazing her body, and the sleeves, too long, cover a portion of her hands. She doesn't smile when she sees me. She seems distracted, and her eyes blaze with apprehension.

"Happy New Year, Mamma."

"You came."

I kiss her forehead and put the water on for tea. And as I arrange the cookies on a plate and prepare the teapot she lists her various aches and pains: a throbbing at the base of her spine, an intermittent pang in her wrist, insomnia, and the results of her latest blood test, which were more or less normal. And as she conveys the details of her precarious health, I, a person who's young compared with her, who's active, who's healthy on the whole, feel instantly disheartened. I'm overcome by the obligation to cure her various ills, to reverse the symptoms of her decline, to enliven that thin, drawn face. That fragile person who continues to breathe, digest food, empty her bowels, and move about, albeit slowly, has by now evolved into an organism more complex than ever, a fact that fills me with awe and also with dread.

I sense she's telling me all this as if to say: Look, I'm full of glitches, defects, hazards that might at any moment plunge me into a state of dramatic decline, that might snatch me away definitively. Prepare yourself, she says every time we see each other. Prepare for the catastrophe.

But is this really what she's telling me? Is she trying to worry me, to scare me? Maybe it's in my head, maybe it's just my own projection. Why do I feel so assailed by what she says? By a string of simple facts? Why do I immediately start to panic? Once again I feel suspended, unable to step between the tree stumps of my childhood, frozen before the precipice. I fear I'm a terrible daughter who ignores her mother, whose fault is to be excessively alive. And yet she's calm, everything's calm, there are no more scenes, no drama, she no longer raises her voice. She talks about herself, she finds no faults with me. She's turned laconic. But oh what rages she'd fly into, when she was my age! I remember days, in summer, when I'd be tempted to get up and close the windows so that the neighbors wouldn't hear her, because I'd blocked that rage inside.

I put the cat's tongues on a plate, arrange the cups and saucers, a porcelain sugar bowl I recognize from childhood. We drink the tea and eat some cookies. She doesn't ask me questions. She asks nothing about my work, my life in the city. We talk about the weather, the news, and watch a little TV together. Then she comments on the lives of other people, her neighbors, their ups and downs, elderly women whose grandchildren come to visit on Sundays. I have to stay poised, if not, her brooding spirit pervades mine.

What does she make of my solitary life, the choices I've made? Would she have liked a couple of grandchildren, an attentive son-in-law? Certainly that's what she had in mind.

We usually go out for a short walk. She holds my hand in an odd way, with an awkward grasp that's always bothersome. But she doesn't feel like going out today, she's tired, the cold looks harsh, she says. I can't bear it, she's nearing her end.

Before leaving I say, "Mamma, we won't see one another for a while."

"Where are you going?"

"I'm going abroad, it's for my work."

"You'll have to go, then."

"We'll talk on the phone."

She doesn't get upset. She only asks, "How far away is it?"

"It's on the other side of the border."

"Maybe I'll come visit you."

I worry she hasn't really understood what I've told her. But then she says, all in one breath, her eyes still blazing: "When you change houses you always lose something. Every move betrays you, it always cheats you somehow. I'm still looking for certain things. That brooch that belonged to my mother, nothing valuable, but it meant something to me. Then there's my old address book. Even though I don't need it anymore, I liked thumbing through it now and then. I'd saved ticket stubs, certain receipts, a small photograph of your father when he was young, before we'd met, what a handsome fellow he was. I look and look but I can't find it. There are days I comb through the whole house hoping to find those things in some drawer I've already opened countless times, or maybe at the bottom of a box in my closet. They're somewhere, of course. Just like the jewels that were stolen from me. Remember that ring, the gold one, a little flashy, that I liked to wear in winter? It had green stones. I'd left it lying in plain sight when I was younger, when there was always so much to do in the course of any given day. Back then it tormented me, I couldn't stand the fact of having lost that ring. But now I think, oh well. Someone else is probably wearing it, or maybe it's for sale somewhere, in some far-off place, maybe the place you're going to. It's not mine anymore, but it's still somewhere, that's what I'm trying to say."

At this point she stops staring at me and starts looking around the room. "Where do you think that address book might be?"

"I don't know, Mamma. It's somewhere, I suppose."

"You think so? Bring some more of these when you come back to see me, they're so tasty," she says, breaking a cat's tongue in two.

At the Station

As I wait for the train that will take me home I ask for a coffee at the station bar. It's run by a couple, they're friendly but reserved. He's wearing a thick heavy sweater the same shade of gray as his bushy eyebrows. His wife looks good for her age, still slim, with a tall, old-fashioned hairdo and a pair of reading glasses hanging from a chain around her neck. They've been husband and wife for half a century. On a shelf behind the counter, among the bottles of spirits, they've displayed the cards they received for their fiftieth anniversary.

The wife prepares my coffee and offers me some whipped cream to stir into the cup. I ask her to warm me a sandwich. But it won't assuage me. The effect of seeing my mother, so debilitated, is always the same. A metaphor comes to mind and I look for a pen in my handbag. I don't have a notebook with me, so I jot this down on the back of a receipt stuck in my wallet: *My mother, by now, clings to life like a yellowing piece of Scotch tape in a scrapbook. It can detach at any moment, and yet it still does the job. All you need to do is turn the page to unstick it, so that it leaves a pale rectangular stain behind.*

I'm not impressed by what I've just written, it feels overwrought, but I hold on to the receipt. I go to pay at the register, taking my place in line. I keep my wallet in my hand but the person who's paying in front of me keeps chatting, and meanwhile there's a train pulling into the station. I didn't expect it quite yet, I've lost track of the time.

"Oh dear, is that my train?" I ask the man who owns the bar.

"It's always on time."

"What should I do?"

"Get on it."

"I'm so sorry—"

"You'd better hurry," he adds.

I run off without saying goodbye to the couple, without saying Happy New Year to anyone. I board the train, dumbfounded, feeling mysteriously protected by the universe, or at least by that man who gave me something to eat and drink without insisting that I pay. Such a kind and unexpected gesture on the first day of the year replenishes me but it also discombobulates, so much so that as I ride home, my eyes brim with tears.

In the Mirror

I clean the house from top to bottom. Every neglected nook and cranny, each windowsill, all the floors, the lampshades. I remove the stains that the detergents leave under the sink and the line of dark dust that creeps on top of the molding, dragging my finger along it, wrapped in a cloth. I clean the inside of the washing machine and the inside of my garbage can. I sweep away the detritus that gathers by the threshold of the balcony. After that I get rid of the lime that encrusts the faucets, submerging the washers in a glass of white vinegar. Now that I'm about to leave this place I want to remove every trace of myself.

I move the furniture around, inspecting within, behind, beneath. This type of filth spreads everywhere, there's no end to it. It works its way into every surface. I go to the hardware store and buy a few things to spruce up the kitchen. Hooks for my pot holders, a receptacle in which my sponges can rest and drain. I toss out the chewed-up wooden spoons and buy new ones, arranging them in a vase like flowers. And as I'm sifting through all my belongings, I come across an old ceramic plate in a closet. Something that broke long ago. It's in two pieces now, each still intact, the smaller one in the shape of a triangle, like a slice cut from a cake. I'm about to toss them out when I change my mind. I'm inspired to join them back up. And I think it would be worth the trouble. It's a hand-painted piece, I'd bought it on vacation in the mountains once. I can't remember when.

I go back to the hardware store and ask for a glue that's good for ceramics. They give me a product that has superpowers, they say, that can make anything stick to anything else. Back at home, seated at my desk, I open the tube, follow the directions, and attach the slice to the rest of the cake. It sets instantly so that I can barely see the crack. It looks like a single folded hair. But when I close the tube I press it by mistake and a sizable clump of glue spurts out, covering my fingers, drying immediately, leaving a stubborn film on my skin. I wash my hands but that just makes matters worse. The water doesn't rinse away the glue, and by now my fingers are sticking to one another as firmly as the slice to the rest of the cake. I look up and see myself in the mirror, weary, stiff hands coated with glue whose ghostly traces resemble the dust I've been working hard to get rid of all day, and after a long time, or maybe for the first time, I burst out laughing.

At the Crypt

I go visit you, too, Papà. I bring you flowers and I hear you ask me, what's the point of these?

Here you are, in the heart of the city, surrounded by the dead: all those souls still wreathed and garlanded, lined up like boxes in the post office. You always occupied your own space. You preferred dwelling in your own realm, closed off. How can I link myself to another person when I'm still struggling, even after your death, to eliminate the distance between you and my mother, the woman with whom you chose, inexplicably, to share a life and have a child? Even today I see you walking three feet ahead of her. And maybe the gaps between those tree stumps I always hoped would diminish, and perhaps even close up completely, represented that space between the two of you.

You, who chafed at the collective we created, who

only wanted to subtract yourself, always, from the equation, throwing it off-balance. You who would say succinctly and plainly while she and I would argue: Why ask me? I have nothing to do with it. You would just repeat those two sentences, a response I found both brutal and cowardly on your part. But as a result I learned not to involve you, and to never expect you to save me.

You had something to do with it, maybe you even had everything to do with it. You still do. You still occupy a space in our family, even more than the space allotted to you now in your little cell. That's why, standing today before your cold compartment, I can't forgive you. I don't forgive you for never having stepped into those arguments, for never protecting me, for having forsaken your role as my defender, all because you felt that you were the victim in that tempestuous household. But that magma never touched you, you'd already built yourself an enclosure that was taller and thicker than the marble that encases you now.

What's it like in a place where it's always dark? You hated when we turned on the lights, you'd go around shutting them off, as often as you could, in all the rooms. You're being wasteful, you'd grumble. On Sunday, when you had no choice but to spend the day with us, when you had no errands or appointments, no means of escape, you'd settle into an armchair in the living room, in a darkness of your own making. That was a waste of time, you'd remark after the fact, if you and my mother happened to quarrel.

You can't go for your solitary walks anymore, you can't go anywhere. You always wanted calm seas. You used to claim you got along with everyone, that you kept to yourself, that you needed nothing from no one. But one can't ask the sea to never swell into rage. And you asked a great deal from me. You asked me to accept your measured responsibility, to acknowledge that you were a devoted father who was never besotted with his child.

A fever out of the blue that started to spike not long after we'd closed our suitcases. We'd already lined them up, one next to the other, in the hallway. We were supposed to leave the following day, early in the morning. But around midnight you began to slip away, your eyes unblinking, filled with fear. The second day, in the hospital, your vital organs had already begun to die.

We were supposed to go see a play together, that was something we did, you and I. The only thing that really excited you. You loved that darkness in particular, and that seat reserved for you and only you, in which you eagerly absorbed the woes of other characters. I refused to unpack my suitcase for a month. I mourned those wasted tickets, and that trip never taken, more than I mourned for you.

Up Ahead

The day before I go I step out into the piazza for a last glimpse of my present surroundings: a cupola turning pink from the setting sun, the big door to a palazzo that contains, at the back of its courtyard, a nude marble woman with arms always raised, her face always turned to one side. I've still got a few errands to run—at the pharmacy, at the dry cleaner, at my seamstress just around the corner. The piazza has emptied out, the farmers have taken down their market tents, and someone has already swept away the cauliflower leaves and the clementines that always fall out of their wooden crates. There are a few older people sitting on benches for a bit of fresh air, a few parents panting after children who have just been sprung free from tiny apartments.

This is the moment in the day when the stores reopen, a moment of transition, and I'm aware of all the people—the kids walking home, exhausted and starved after a hectic day of high school; that smiling man, small in stature, who walks an enormous dog with a white woolly coat that covers his eyes; the half-blind guy who panhandles outside the bar—who aren't leaving to go anywhere, who will remain right here. They'll keep walking along these sidewalks. They're permanent fixtures in my mind, knotted up in the fabric of my neighborhood just like the buildings, the trees, the marble woman. These are the faces that have kept me company for years, and I still don't even know the people they belong to. There's no point saying goodbye to them, or adding, we'll meet again, even though right now I'm overflowing with affection for each of them.

As I walk and turn sad at the thought of soon leaving this place, I see another person out of the corner of my eye: a woman, walking at the other end of the block, dressed almost exactly as I am. She, too, wears a wide red skirt flecked with black threads. A woolen coat, black like mine, tall boots, a woolen cap on her head. She, too, carries her bag over her right shoulder. I have no idea how old she is, she could be my age or fifteen years older, or maybe she's just a girl. She's got a sprightly step, she clearly knows where she's going.

I ignore the things I need to do and start following her, I have no choice in the matter. I adjust my pace, speeding up a bit, then wait while she pauses at the crosswalk. I wonder if anyone else on the street remarks on the coincidence of two women, twinned, strangers to one another, who walk together, also separately. What's her face like? Has she always lived here, like me? Or is she just visiting? If so, why? Is she meeting someone? Is it something for work? Is she going to visit her grandmother, a woman in a wheelchair who can no longer come downstairs and sit in the piazza? Is she a woman with millions of things to do? Is she anxious or carefree? Married or alone? Is she going to ring the buzzer of a friend of hers? A lover? Is she going to stop to drink some fruit juice or have a gelato?

My double, seen from behind, explains something to me: that I'm me and also someone else, that I'm leaving and also staying. This realization momentarily jostles my melancholy, like a current that stirs the branches, that discomfits the leaves of a tree.

I wait until she crosses the street, then keep following. There's no traffic light here, I need to wait for a clearing. The road has a slight curve up ahead, and for an instant I lose her. I wonder which way to turn. But once I cross to the other side I don't see her, neither to the right nor to the left, nor up ahead. I run toward the piazza and look for her in the gelato shop, in the pharmacy, at the dry cleaner. I make a round of the whole piazza, searching for her, as if she were the morning paper I'd just bought at the newsstand, still to unfold, the sheets still smooth and clean, left mistakenly by the cash register while I was paying for my coffee at the bar. I can get distracted that way. I always end up finding the newspaper again, the store owner in question always sets it aside for me. But I've lost her, she's gone.

Did I imagine her? No, I'm certain I saw her. A variation of myself with a sprightly step, determined to get somewhere, just up ahead.

Nowhere

Because when all is said and done the setting doesn't matter: the space, the walls, the light. It makes no difference whether I'm under a clear blue sky or caught in the rain or swimming in the transparent sea in summer. I could be riding a train or traveling by a car or flying in a plane, among the clouds that drift and spread on all sides like a mass of jellyfish in the air. I've never stayed still, I've always been moving, that's all I've ever been doing. Always waiting either to get somewhere or to come back. Or to escape. I keep packing and unpacking the small suitcase at my feet. I hold my purse in my lap, it's got some money and a book to read. Is there any place we're not moving through? *Disoriented, lost, at sea, at odds, astray, adrift, bewildered, confused, uprooted, turned around.* I'm related to these related terms. These words are my abode, my only foothold.

On the Train

There are five of them, four men and a woman, all more or less the same age. They resemble one another strongly, they've all got dark hair, some meat on their bones, and they smile easily. The woman says hello before taking her place across from me, beside the window. And in a heartbeat, my compartment on the train, where I'd been quietly reading, thrums with energy. I can't figure out how they're related to each other. Are they siblings? Cousins? Three brothers and a couple? Or just five friends who behave as if they were a family?

As soon as they've boarded and settled into their seats they start eating, they all appear to be starved. On the table between them they open up a series of bags filled with healthy but tasty food: walnuts, blood oranges, dried figs, all of which they quickly devour. They share these comestibles, placing wedges of fruit and pieces of chocolate into each other's mouths as if they were all mothers, and also all children eager to be fed. There's such affection coursing between them. What zeal for life, how pleased they are to be together. They appear to need nothing more.

They're talking the whole time in a language I don't recognize. I take it as a sign—soon enough I'll be in another country, surrounded by another impenetrable tongue. As they converse they listen to music—songs filled with pain and passion—on one of their cell phones. The sound quality is awful but the music overwhelms them. They close their eyes and react to it. Now and then they sing along, as if it were perfectly normal to sing out loud on a train full of strangers.

They offer me the walnuts, the figs, the chocolates, the blood oranges. All the food looks fresh, appealing. But I'm not hungry, I've already eaten a sandwich, tasteless and rather cold.

The group's effusive behavior clashes with that of the other passengers. Not one of them reads a book, or naps, or talks softly on a cell phone. They shatter the silence, they disrupt the monotony of the trip. This boisterous crew transforms the atmosphere of the train I'll be sitting in all day long.

I wonder where they're going. All the way to the last stop, in order to reach the border and then cross it, like me? They appear to be waiting for something, they're excited, also a bit nervous. Every time the train makes a stop they look outside, alert, as if they don't know whether or not they should be getting off. Who are they going to see? What's the occasion? What's about to happen in these people's lives?

The woman, who's wearing quite a bit of makeup, has a round face and large, flashing dark eyes. She reacts to the music, uninhibited, and at one point, noticing that she's in tears, I look the other way. Then she starts to teach one of her companions how to say goodbye in our language. She repeats it again and again, and they all start laughing. As if there were schoolchildren they recite, together, *ar-ri-ve-der-ci!*

Then without warning one of the men turns into a hairdresser. He pulls the equipment out of his backpack: a brush, a curling iron, linseed oil, spray. He gives the woman a very elaborate hairdo. As he brushes and styles her hair the others take numerous photos of her, to document each step of the process.

The others aren't formally dressed. Short leather jackets, dark pants, sneakers.

She rests her sunglasses on the table, next to the hard-shell case that contains my reading glasses. Her pair is made of cheap plastic and the lenses are scratched, like wrinkles on a forehead or like the folds of the sea if you see it from very far away or from

up high. My lenses are costly, polished smooth. Her laughter is frequent, it pours from her seductively. She tells various stories, long detailed anecdotes to entertain the others. They listen to her, transfixed.

A plastic garbage bag sits at their feet, among all the backpacks, and by now it's bulging with orange peels that need to be thrown away. They've torn through all the food, nothing of what they brought to eat on board remains.

At the next stop, they get up abruptly. They say goodbye to me, thank me, apologize. Then they grab their things and get off. They leave me in my place, with my book, my hard-shell eyeglass case, my lightly packed suitcase.

There's no more trace of the foreign brigade, that feeding frenzy. The table is spotless, the seats they'd just occupied are again free. Now I regret not having accepted even a morsel of their lavish meal. But thanks to them, not even a crumb of it lingers.

Notes

Page 77: *Portagioie,* the Italian word for jewelry box, is a compound of two polyvalent words. *Gioia* (pl. *gioie*) means both "joy" and "jewel." *Porta,* meanwhile, derives from the Latin verb *portāre,* and belongs to a constellation of words pertaining to acts of bearing, bringing, carrying, and transporting, which in turn give rise to terms for "door," "gate," and "port." *Porta-gioie,* therefore, could also be interpreted, in Italian, not only as a box of jewels, but a container of joy, a doorway or gateway to joy, something that brings joy.

The quotation on page 123 comes from *Il mare* (The sea) by Corrado Alvaro:

Io, dopo un poco, fuggo interrorito all'ombra dalla grande fiamma: mi sembra debba consumarmi, che mi prenda e mi riduca un elemento ancor più piccolo

di questa terra, un verme o una pianta . . . Non riesco
a pensare a nulla, tutto mi sembra inutile, la vita mi
appare d'una facilità estrema, non m'importa se di
me non si occupa più nessuno, se quasi più nessuno
mi scrive.

THE CLOTHING OF BOOKS

How do you clothe a book? In this deeply personal reflection, Pulitzer Prize–winning author Jhumpa Lahiri explores the art of the book jacket from the perspectives of both reader and writer. Probing the complex relationships between text and image, author and designer, and art and commerce, Lahiri delves into the role of the uniform; explains what book jackets and design have come to mean to her; and shares how, sometimes, "the covers become a part of me."

Literary Criticism

IN OTHER WORDS

On a post-college visit to Florence, Pulitzer Prize–winning author Jhumpa Lahiri fell in love with the Italian language. Twenty years later, seeking total immersion, she and her family relocated to Rome, where she began to read and write solely in her adopted tongue. A startling act of self-reflection, *In Other Words* is Lahiri's meditation on the process of learning to express herself in another language—and the stunning journey of a writer seeking a new voice.

Memoir

THE LOWLAND

The Lowland is an engrossing family saga steeped in history: the story of two very different brothers bound by tragedy, a fiercely brilliant woman haunted by her past, a country torn apart by revolution, and a love that endures long past death. Moving from the 1960s to the present, and from India to America and across generations, this dazzling novel is Jhumpa Lahiri at the height of her considerable powers.

Fiction

The eight stories in *Unaccustomed Earth* take us from Cambridge and Seattle to India and Thailand, as they explore the secrets at the heart of family life. They enter the worlds of sisters and brothers, fathers and mothers, daughters and sons, friends and lovers. Rich with the signature gifts that have established Jhumpa Lahiri as one of our most essential writers, *Unaccustomed Earth* exquisitely renders the most intricate workings of the heart and mind.

Fiction

VINTAGE CONTEMPORARIES
Available wherever books are sold.
www.vintagebooks.com